ERIC M. ATTIO

Wine & Wisdom

First edition

ISBN: 978-1-969453-00-7

This book was professionally typeset on Reedsy. Find out more at reedsy.com

Contents

Wine & Wisdom

By Eric M. Attio
© 2025

PRONUNCIATION GUIDE

Note: *Chinese pronunciation varies by region and historical period. These approximations are designed to help English readers navigate the text comfortably while respecting the original sounds.*

THE PROTAGONIST'S JOURNEY

- **Li Xiuyuan → Brother Daoji → Ji Gong** *This name progression reflects the protagonist's spiritual transformation throughout the novel: from privileged youth to institutional monk to free agent of compassion*
- **Li Xiuyuan** - *lee shee-yu-ahn* The protagonist's birth name; "Cultivating Excellence"
- **Daoji** - *dao-jee* The protagonist's monastic name; "The Way of Compassion"
- **Ji Gong** - *jee gong* The protagonist's common name; "Lord of Compassion"

FAMILY & ORIGINS

- **Li Maolin** - *lee mao-lin* Xiuyuan's father; wealthy merchant
- **Lady Song** - *song* Xiuyuan's mother; from aristocratic family

RELIGIOUS FIGURES

- **Master Hui** - *hway* Buddhist monk and Ji Gong's teacher; "Wisdom"
- **Abbot Yuan Kong** - *yu-ahn kong* Head of Lingyin Temple; "Perfect Emptiness"
- **Brother Wuxin** - *woo-shin* Temple administrator; "No Mind"
- **Brother An** - *ahn* Elder monk; "Peace"
- **Brother Shi** - *shee* Temple monk; "Stone"
- **Brother Jing** - *jing* Senior monk; "Tranquil"
- **Brother Bai** - *bye* Temple monk; "White"

GOVERNMENT OFFICIALS

- **Magistrate Wang Jinshan** - *wahng jin-shahn* Local administrator; "Golden Mountain Wang"
- **Governor Shen Shimin** - *shen shee-min* Provincial governor; "Benefiting the People"
- **Liu Ming** - *lee-oo ming* Government secretary; "Bright"
- **Captain Song Hu** - *song hoo* Military officer; "Song Tiger"

SCHOLARS & STUDENTS

- **Scholar Wen Zhiming** - *when zhee-ming* Academy instructor; "Cultured and Bright"
- **Wei Sin** - *way sin* Young scholar; "Renewal"
- **Li Hua** - *lee hwah* Silk weaver; "Beautiful Flower"
- **Zhang Ming** - *jahng ming* Student; "Bright Zhang"
- **Ren Zixuan** - *ren zee-shoo-ahn* Student; "Self-Chosen"

MOUNTAIN FOLK (Former Bandits)

- **Old Tiger** - *(English name)* Mountain leader; formerly Squad Leader Liang
- **Squad Leader Liang** - *lee-ahng* Old Tiger's real name; "brilliant"
- **Iron Wolf** - *(English name)* Former blacksmith
- **Stone** - *(English name)* Former farmer
- **Gray Fox** - *(English name)* Former merchant's guard
- **Young Crane** - *(English name)* Young bandit
- **Viper** - *(English name)* Old Tiger's lieutenant

MERCHANTS & CITIZENS

- **Master Zhao** - *zhao* Textile merchant
- **Zhao Weiming** - *zhao way-ming* Young merchant
- **Master Bo** - *boh* Silk merchant
- **Widow Tan** - *tahn* Market vendor; sells vegetables
- **Dong** - *dong* Tavern keeper of the Drunken Phoenix
- **Mu** - *moo* Carpenter
- **Yan** - *yahn* Blacksmith
- **Captain Wu** - *woo* Former soldier, now dock worker

- **Widow Su** - *soo* Seamstress
- **Jingfei** - *jing-fay* Mother of young children
- **Jun** - *jun* Guard

PLACES

- **Hangzhou** - *hahng-joe* Major city in southern China; Song Dynasty capital
- **Lingyin Temple** - *ling-yin* Buddhist monastery; "Soul's Retreat"
- **Zhejiang Province** - *zheh-jee-ahng* Regional setting in eastern China
- **Guangzhou** - *gwahng-joe* Southern trading city
- **Deqing** - *duh-ching* Village
- **Moon Ridge** – *(Translation)* Mountain location

CULTURAL & RELIGIOUS TERMS

- **Li** - *lee* Unit of distance (approximately 1/3 mile)
- **Dao** - *dao* Curved sword
- **Guanyin** - *gwahn-yin* Buddhist Goddess of Mercy and Compassion
- **Xuanzang** - *shoo-ahn-zahng* Historical Buddhist monk (602-664 CE)
- **Dharma** - *dar-mah* Buddhist teaching and cosmic law
- **Sangha** - *sahng-gah* Buddhist community of monks and nuns
- **Dukkha** - *doo-kah* Buddhist concept of suffering and dissatisfaction
- **Tanha** - *tahn-hah* Craving and attachment that causes suffering

- **Nirodha** - *nee-roh-dah* Cessation of suffering
- **Magga** - *mahg-gah* The Noble Eightfold Path
- **Bodhisattva** - *boh-dee-saht-vah* Enlightened being who helps others achieve liberation
- **Karma** - *kar-mah* Law of cause and effect; moral consequences of actions
- **Samsara** - *sahm-sah-rah* Cycle of birth, death, and rebirth

FOOD & DAILY ITEMS

- **Congee** - *kon-jee* Rice porridge, often eaten for breakfast
- **Baozi** - *bow-dzuh* Steamed buns with various fillings
- **Weiqi** - *way-chee* Strategic board game (known as "Go" in the West)
- **Joss sticks** - *(English term)* Incense sticks burned in religious ceremonies

TITLES & HONORIFICS

- **Master** - *shee-foo* Respectful title for teachers, craftsmen, or experts
- **Brother** - *shee-sheong* Term for fellow monks or students
- **Venerable** - *dzun-juh* Honorific for senior religious figures
- **Honored** - *dzun-jing-duh* Polite address for respected persons
- **Old** - *lao* Respectful prefix for elders (as in "Old Tiger")

PRONUNCIATION NOTES

- **Tone Variations**: Chinese is a tonal language, but these approximations focus on consonant and vowel sounds rather than tones
- **Regional Differences**: Song Dynasty pronunciation differed from modern Mandarin; these guides represent accessible approximations
- **"zh" Sound**: Pronounced like "j" in "judge"
- **"x" Sound**: Pronounced like "sh" in "she"
- **"q" Sound**: Pronounced like "ch" in "cheese"
- **Final "ng"**: As in "song" or "ring"
- **"ü" Sound**: Like German "ü" or French "u"; approximate with "ew" as in "few"

These pronunciations prioritize accessibility for English readers while maintaining respect for the original Chinese sounds. When in doubt, the meaning and story matter more than perfect pronunciation.

Dedication

To Ji Gong, whose wisdom transcends centuries,
to my family & friends, who believed
in this story before it was written,
and to all who find the sacred in the ordinary.

Author's Note

Ji Gong, also known as Dao Ji, was a real Buddhist monk who lived during the Southern Song Dynasty (1130-1209 CE). Born Li Xiuyuan into a wealthy family, he became one of the most beloved figures in Chinese folklore, known for his unconventional approach to Buddhist teaching and his compassion for common people.

The historical Ji Gong was famous for breaking monastic rules in service of a higher compassion: drinking wine, eating meat, and living among the poor while demonstrating profound wisdom and reportedly performing miracles. His story has been told and retold for over eight hundred years through countless folk tales, operas, novels, and films, each generation finding new meaning in his radical approach to spirituality and social justice.

This novel is a work of fiction inspired by the legendary Ji Gong. While I have drawn from traditional stories and historical context, the specific events, dialogue, and many of the characters in this book are products of my imagination. I have taken creative liberties with historical details to serve the narrative, and my interpretation of Ji Gong's philosophy reflects my own understanding rather than any authoritative religious doctrine.

The themes explored here (the tension between institutional order and individual conscience, the power of compassion to transform communities, and the idea that true wisdom often appears as foolishness to conventional thinking) are as relevant today as they were in twelfth-century China. In our current era of social division and institutional mistrust, Ji Gong's example offers a timeless reminder that genuine change begins not with grand reforms but with simple acts of human kindness.

I have endeavored to treat both the historical figure and the cultural traditions surrounding him with respect, while creating a story that speaks to contemporary readers about the enduring power of love over fear, wisdom over convention, and hope over cynicism.

For readers interested in learning more about the historical Ji Gong and traditional Chinese Buddhist philosophy, I encourage exploration of primary sources and scholarly works on Chinese religious history.

Any errors in historical detail or cultural representation are my own, and I apologize in advance for any inadvertent mischaracterizations of this rich and complex tradition.

Eric M. Attio

Chapter 1

The Golden Cage

Southern Song Dynasty, 12th Century China

The morning sun painted the Li family courtyard in shades of amber and gold, its light dancing across the polished surfaces of carved jade ornaments and silk tapestries that adorned every corner of their mansion. Young Li Xiuyuan sat cross-legged on a cushion of yellow brocade, his dark eyes fixed not on the calligraphy scroll before him, but on the sparrows that had gathered outside the latticed window, pecking at scattered rice grains left by the kitchen servants.

"Concentrate, young master," urged Master Bao, his voice carrying the patience of a man who had tutored the sons of wealthy families for twenty-one years. "The character for 'virtue' requires perfect balance between strength and grace."

The task before Xiuyuan was a classical poem by Du Fu, each character requiring precise brushstrokes that would demonstrate not only his calligraphy skills but his understanding of proper literary form. The ink stone beside him had been ground from precious Duan stone, its surface worn smooth by generations of Li family scholars. Around the study, red lacquered cabinets held scrolls of poetry, histories of the Han and Tang dynasties, and treatises on Confucian governance that his father expected him to master before taking his place in the family business.

Xiuyuan's brush hovered over the rice paper, a drop of black ink trembling at its tip like a tear about to fall. At seventeen, he possessed the refined features of his noble lineage. These included high cheekbones, intelligent eyes, and hands that had never known calluses or want.

Yet something restless stirred beneath his composed exterior, like a caged bird beating its wings against invisible bars. The restlessness had been growing for months, fed by fragments of Buddhist sutras he'd read in secret and conversations with traveling merchants who spoke of places where helping others brought more respect than hoarding riches. He'd begun to notice things that had once been invisible: how the servants' children wore patched clothes while he owned dozens of silk robes, how the kitchen servants ate rice gruel while he complained about the quality of his gourmet meals.

Late at night, he would lie awake wondering if the philosophical texts he studied had any meaning beyond academic exercise.

"Master Bao," Xiuyuan said softly, setting down his brush, "why do we practice writing 'virtue' when outside our gates, children beg for the rice we waste?"

The tutor's eyebrows rose like startled caterpillars. In all his years of service, no student had asked such a question. "Young master, it is... it is not our place to question the natural order.

Your father's success in trade has blessed your family. The poor have their own karma to work through."

Xiuyuan turned back to the window, where the sparrows had finished their meager feast and taken flight. "But what if our karma and theirs are connected, Master Bao? What if my full rice bowl creates their empty one?"

Before his tutor could formulate a response, the sound of approaching footsteps echoed through the marble corridors. Li Maolin, Xiuyuan's father, entered the study with the measured stride of a man accustomed to authority. His silk robes rustled with the soft elegance of wealth, and the jade rings on his fingers caught the morning light.

Xiuyuan's mother, Lady Song, rarely appeared during his lessons, but her influence shaped the household like subtle incense. She had been born to a family of imperial court officials, and her expectations for her son included not just commercial success but social refinement that would elevate the Li family's status beyond mere wealth. In her private conversations with Xiuyuan, she spoke of duty to family honor, of the sacrifices previous generations had made, and of his obligation to marry well and produce heirs who would carry their name even higher.

"How progresses my son's education?" Maolin asked, though his eyes were already scanning the barely touched calligraphy exercise.

"Your son shows great... scholarly curiosity," Master Bao replied carefully, his diplomatic training evident in every word.

Maolin's gaze shifted to Xiuyuan, who had risen and bowed respectfully. "Philosophy feeds neither family nor business, my son."

This wasn't the first time Xiuyuan's questions had troubled

his tutors. As a child, he had asked why some families lived in grand compounds while others slept in doorways. At twelve, he had tried to give his New Year money to a beggar and been sharply corrected. At fifteen, he had suggested the family open their private granary during a famine and been sent to his room without dinner. Each incident had been dismissed as childhood softness that he would outgrow, but Maolin was beginning to realize his son's compassion might be a permanent flaw in his character.

"Come, I have news that will interest you more than dusty scrolls."

They walked together through the gardens, past ornamental ponds where golden carp swam in lazy circles, their movements as predictable as the seasons. Servants tended to every flower, every stone carefully placed to create perfect harmony. Yet to Xiuyuan, the beauty felt hollow, like an exquisite mask hiding something essential.

"The magistrate has agreed to our proposal," Maolin announced, his chest swelling with pride. "The new trade route through Guangzhou will make us one of the wealthiest families in all of Zhejiang province. Your future is secured, my son. Your children's future is secured."

Xiuyuan paused beside a stone bridge that arched gracefully over a stream of clear water. Below, he could see his reflection wavering in the current, distorted and uncertain. "Father, yesterday I walked beyond our gates…"

"You did what?" Maolin's voice sharpened like a blade being drawn.

"I wanted to see the market, to understand the world beyond our walls. I saw an old woman collapse from hunger, right there in the street. People stepped around her as if she were a stone."

She had been carrying a bundle of thin vegetables, probably all she could afford. When she fell, the vegetables spilled across the cobblestones, and rather than helping her, people scrambled to claim the scattered food. Xiuyuan had started forward, but his escort pulled him back, warning of disease and desperation. By the time his carriage moved on, she was still lying there. The image had burned itself into his mind.

Maolin's jaw tightened. "The world outside these walls is dangerous and dirty, Xiuyuan. That is precisely why we maintain our position to protect ourselves and our family from such suffering."

"But should we not try to end the suffering itself, rather than simply avoid it?"

For a moment, father and son stood in silence, the gentle splash of the ornamental stream the only sound between them. When Maolin spoke again, his words heavy with generational authority.

"Your great-grandfather built this fortune grain by grain, trading silk and tea along the dangerous mountain passes. Your grandfather expanded it, surviving wars and famines that destroyed lesser families. I have made it flourish beyond their wildest dreams. This is your inheritance, Xiuyuan: security, respect, power. Do not throw it away for romantic notions about saving the world."

That evening, as incense burned in the family shrine and his parents performed their ritual prayers to the ancestors, Xiuyuan stood on his balcony watching the lights of the city below. The family shrine occupied the place of honor in the main hall, its carved sandalwood panels depicting scenes from classical mythology. Portraits of Li ancestors gazed down with painted eyes, their silk robes and jade ornaments speaking of centuries of accumulated prosperity. His mother knelt before offerings of rice wine, fresh fruit, and burning joss sticks, her lips moving in prayers for the family's continued success. The ritual had remained unchanged for generations: gratitude to those who had built their fortune, and requests for their blessing on future endeavors. Each flickering flame represented a family, a story, struggles and joys he would never know from within his golden prison.

The scent of jasmine drifted up from the gardens, sweet and intoxicating. In the distance, he could hear the faint sound of laughter from a tavern where common people gathered, their simple pleasures unmarked by the burden of great wealth.

A strange thought formed in his mind, fragile as a soap bubble yet persistent as the evening stars: What if true security came not from building higher walls, but from tearing them down? What if real power lay not in accumulating wealth, but in giving it away?

For hours, Xiuyuan wrestled with possibilities that seemed impossible. How could he abandon everything his family had built? How could he turn his back on the security and comfort that so many envied? Yet how could he continue to live surrounded by luxury while pretending not to see the suffering that luxury was built upon? He thought of the Buddhist teaching he had read in secret: that all suffering was connected, that no one could be truly free while others remained in bondage. The words had seemed like beautiful philosophy then, but tonight they felt like a call to action he could no longer ignore.

As the moon rose over the tiled roofs of Hangzhou, young Li Xiuyuan made a decision that would echo through the centuries, though he did not yet know the name by which history would remember him: Ji Gong, the Crazy Monk who chose compassion over comfort, wisdom over wealth, and the boundless freedom of spirit over the beautiful cage of worldly success. Tomorrow, he would walk through the temple gates not as a visitor, but as someone seeking a different kind of inheritance entirely. The sparrows he had watched that morning were already asleep in their nests, dreaming perhaps of tomorrow's scattered rice. But their wings, at least, knew no barriers save the sky itself.

Chapter 2

The Temple Gates

Six months later, the first autumn rains drummed against the curved eaves of Lingyin Temple like the urgent fingers of a restless spirit. The weathered monastery perched on the hillside carved from stone and timber in perfect meditation, its weathered walls having witnessed countless seasons of seeking souls.

Xiuyuan knelt in the temple's main hall before the towering statue of Guanyin, the Goddess of Mercy, whose serene face seemed to glow in the flickering candlelight. The sacred space enveloped him in an atmosphere thick as morning mist. Sandalwood incense spiraled upward from bronze braziers, carrying the prayers of generations skyward. The soft click of wooden prayer beads marked the rhythm of meditation, while gray-robed monks moved like gentle shadows between pillars of carved pine. Above, glazed roof tiles caught fragments of sunlight, casting amber patterns across walls adorned with silk banners bearing sutras written in elegant gold calligraphy. Here, surrounded by the accumulated devotion of generations, even breathing felt like prayer. He had been coming here in secret for weeks, drawn by something he could not name. It was a pull stronger than duty and deeper than curiosity.

"Young master Li," came a gentle voice behind him. "You return to us again."

Xiuyuan turned to see Master Hui approaching, his gray robes whispering against the polished floor. The old monk's face was a map of kindness, lined with years of compassion and understanding. Unlike the temple's other residents, who treated the wealthy merchant's son with careful deference, Hui spoke to him as simply another seeker.

"Master, I... I find peace here that I cannot find elsewhere," Xiuyuan admitted, rising from his knees. "At home, everything is planned, predetermined. Here, I feel as though I might discover who I truly am."

Hui's eyes crinkled with the hint of a smile. "And who do you think you truly are, young master?"

The question hung in the air like the temple bell's resonance after its final strike. Xiuyuan had asked himself the same thing countless times during these clandestine visits, watching the monks go about their daily routines of prayer, meditation, and simple service.

As he knelt on the cold stone floor, Xiuyuan's body remembered the silk-sheeted bed he had left that morning, the soft cushions that had never known the ache of prolonged prayer. His breakfast had been warm congee with preserved eggs and delicate vegetables arranged like flowers on porcelain dishes worth more than most families earned in a season. Yet here, his stomach clenched not with hunger but with shame. How many mornings had he complained that his tea was too weak, his rice too plain, while outside these very gates people dreamed of such abundance? His hands, soft from a lifetime of never knowing work, trembled as he pressed them together in supplication. He pushed these thoughts aside as he focused on Hui's question.

"I don't know," he said finally. "But I know who I'm not. I'm not the merchant prince my father envisions. I'm not content to spend my life accumulating more of what we already have in abundance while others lack even the basic necessities."

"And what would you do instead?"

Before Xiuyuan could answer, hurried footsteps echoed through the hall. A young novice monk rushed in, his face flushed with exertion.

"Master Hui," the boy gasped, "there's a crowd gathering at the temple gates. They're… they're angry."

They could hear voices rising in heated discussion, punctuated by occasional shouts. Hui's expression grew grave as they walked together toward the entrance, Xiuyuan following despite the monk's gentle suggestion that he remain behind.

Outside the temple gates, perhaps fifty people had gathered: farmers with dirt under their fingernails, laborers with calloused hands, mothers clutching thin children to their sides. Their clothes were patched and faded, their faces drawn with the kind of exhaustion that comes not from a day's work, but from years of struggle.

Among the desperate faces, Xiuyuan began to see individuals rather than a mass of suffering. An elderly grandmother held a feverish child against her chest, the little one's labored breathing telling its own story of illness that claimed so many when the cold winds came. A man with only one arm gently supported his pregnant wife as she swayed with exhaustion, his missing limb a testament to past battles. Two young boys, no more than seven years old, sat with the terrible stillness of children who had learned not to hope for food that would not come. The air held more than the scent of unwashed bodies; it carried the weight of fear and the bitter smell of sickness left to fester without remedy.

At the center of the crowd stood a man Xiuyuan recognized: Yan the blacksmith, whose forge sat near the city's main market. His powerful frame was bent not just with grief but with the weight of a father's helplessness. His hands, scarred from years at the forge, shook as he spoke of his daughter's fever that had raged for three days, burning away her laughter and leaving only weak whimpers. He recognized the young nobleman immediately. Everyone in the district knew the Li family's only son, but desperation had driven him beyond considerations of social propriety.

"Where is your compassion now, holy monks?" Yan called out, his voice breaking. "My daughter lies dying of fever, and the district physician demands more silver than I earn in a year. Yet you sit in your golden temple, surrounded by treasures that could feed a village!"

Through the great doors, the crowd could glimpse the temple's accumulated wealth: a golden Buddha statue that caught the light like captured sunlight, jade ornaments carved by master craftsmen whose names were legends, silk banners embroidered with threads of silver and gold. The bronze incense burners alone could have fed families for months, their intricate dragons and phoenixes dancing in metalwork that represented lifetimes of devotion. Yet these treasures served the spirit, not the body, and temple law forbade their conversion to mere coin, no matter how great the suffering outside the gates.

Voices of agreement rippled through the crowd. A woman stepped forward, her baby thin and quiet against her chest.

"My milk has dried up because I haven't eaten in three days," she said, her voice barely above a whisper. "The rice merchant raised his prices again. He says times are hard, but his warehouses are full while our children starve."

Xiuyuan felt something crack open inside his chest, like ice breaking under the weight of spring floods. These weren't the faceless poor he had observed from his family's carriage, these were individuals, each carrying a burden of suffering that his privileged life had never prepared him to witness.

With measured steps, Master Hui approached, hands neatly joined in silent homage. "My friends, your pain is our pain. The temple has little coin, but we have rice and vegetables. Please, take what you need."

From the temple's shadowed doorways, other monks watched with expressions ranging from sympathy to barely concealed alarm. Brother Wuxin, the temple's senior administrator, stood with his hands pressed together in prayer, but his eyes calculated the cost of feeding fifty desperate people against their limited stores. Whispers passed between the younger monks: "If we give to these, how many more will come tomorrow?" "The Provincial Governor expects temples to maintain order, not encourage begging." "Master Hui should send them to the magistrate." Only Master Hui seemed unmoved by such considerations, his aged face holding only the infinite patience of one who had learned that compassion was not a budget item.

"Rice and vegetables won't pay for medicine," Yan replied bitterly. "Rice and vegetables won't buy justice from corrupt magistrates who favor those with gold over those with empty hands."

"No," Hui agreed quietly. "But perhaps they will keep your daughter alive long enough for us to find another way."

When the monks emerged with baskets of food, Xiuyuan found himself drawn forward by a power beyond his understanding. He reached into his sleeve and withdrew a small silk pouch. It was his monthly allowance, enough silver to buy Yan's daughter the finest physicians in the province.

"Wait," he called out, extending the pouch toward the blacksmith. "For your daughter's medicine."

The crowd fell silent. Yan stared at the young nobleman as if he were a spirit from another realm.

"Are you sure?" Yan asked suspiciously. "What do you want in return?"

Xiuyuan looked into the man's eyes: his expression showed the fierce love of a father willing to fight heaven itself for his child's life, and felt the last of his old world crumble away.

"I want nothing," he said, pressing the silver into Yan's calloused palm. "I want to understand what it means to be truly human."

Later that evening, after the crowd had dispersed and the temple had returned to its customary quiet, Xiuyuan sat with Master Hui in the meditation garden. Cherry blossoms drifted down around them like snow, their brief beauty a reminder of life's precious fragility.

"Your father will not be pleased when he discovers your absence today," Hui observed gently.

"My father believes that virtue is something you practice in the safety of your own gardens," Xiuyuan replied. "I'm beginning to think that real virtue can only be practiced in the world, among those who need it most."

"And what will you do with this understanding?"

Xiuyuan was quiet for a long moment, watching the last of the day's light fade behind the temple's ancient walls. When he spoke, his voice carried a certainty that surprised even him.

"I want to take vows, Master. I want to become a monk."

Hui's eyebrows rose slightly. "The path of a monk is not an escape from the world's problems, young master. It is a deeper engagement with them, but on terms that few understand."

"Then teach me to understand."

The old monk studied Xiuyuan's face in the gathering dusk, seeing perhaps something that others had missed: a restless compassion that could not be contained by conventional wisdom, a spirit too large for any cage, even one made of gold.

"Very well," Hui said at last. "But know this: once you step through these gates as more than a visitor, you can never truly go back. The world will see you differently, expect different things. And you will see yourself differently too."

"The ceremony will be simple," Hui continued gently. "You will take the Three Refuges - formally placing your trust in the Buddha as teacher, his dharma as your guide, and our sangha as your spiritual family. You will receive the precepts that govern a monk's conduct, and choose a dharma name - a new identity that represents your spiritual rebirth. Xiuyuan the merchant's son will become Brother... what name calls to you?"

The young man considered. "Daoji," he said. "The Way of Compassion."

"Brother Daoji," Hui repeated, testing the sound. "Yes. That suits you well."

As if summoned by destiny itself, the temple bell began to toll the evening hour, its bronze voice carrying across the hillside and down into the city below, where Yan the blacksmith knelt beside his daughter's bed, whispering prayers of gratitude to whatever gods or spirits had sent an angel in silk robes to save his child's life.

High above, in the Li family mansion, Li Maolin stood at his son's empty chamber, holding the silk robes Xiuyuan had left folded on his bed. The servants continued lighting lanterns throughout the house, but the young master they sought had already begun his journey toward a different kind of illumination entirely.

Chapter 3

Breaking the Rules

Nine months had passed since Li Xiuyuan became Brother Daoji of Lingyin Temple, trading his silk robes for rough hemp cloth and his soft bed for a wooden plank. The transformation should have been jarring, yet he felt more at peace than ever before. The hemp robes that had once felt rough against his skin now seemed like the most natural clothing in the world. His hands, once soft from a lifetime of privilege, had developed calluses from temple work that he wore like badges of honor. Yet sometimes, in quiet moments like this, memories of his former life would surface unbidden: the weight of silk against his skin, the taste of delicate tea served in porcelain cups, the sound of servants moving quietly through corridors designed never to disturb a master's contemplation. The contrast with his current life wasn't painful. It brought understanding, like comparing shadows to sunlight. This was until the morning he discovered what the temple's evening meal truly cost.

Brother Wuxin, one of the temple's senior administrators,

emerged from the storage room carrying ledgers thick with calculations. His thin face bore the perpetual worry of a man trying to stretch rice grains into miracles. Behind him, through the open door, Daoji glimpsed sacks of grain, jars of oil, and preserved vegetables. It was enough food to feed twice their number.

Brother Wuxin had not always been a man obsessed with numbers and regulations. In his youth, he had been as idealistic as any novice, believing that pure intention could overcome any practical obstacle. But twenty years of managing temple resources through droughts, floods, and the caprice of imperial favor had taught him harsh lessons about the difference between compassion and sustainability. He had seen temples fail when their generosity exceeded their means, watched communities of monks scatter when donations dried up and stores ran empty. His ledgers and calculations weren't cruelty. They were the mathematics of survival in a world that didn't always reward virtue.

The morning bells had rung for the first prayers an hour before dawn, calling the community to their dawn meditation. Now the temple buzzed with quiet activity as monks moved through their prescribed routines: sweeping courtyards with bamboo brooms, tending the vegetable gardens that helped sustain the community, and copying sutras in the scriptorium where the soft scratch of brushes on paper created its own meditation.

The scent of sandalwood incense drifted from the main hall, where several brothers knelt in silent contemplation before beginning their work assignments.

"Brother Daoji," Wuxin called, his words sharp with un-wavering authority. "Master Hui requests your presence in the meditation hall."

But Daoji's attention had shifted to the sounds of the crowd beyond the temple's kitchen courtyard. Peering over the wall, he saw a familiar sight that now struck him differently than it had in his days as a wealthy merchant's son. A line of beggars waited outside the temple's rear gate. This was the same gate where leftover rice was distributed each evening, but only after the monks had eaten their fill.

Among them stood an old woman he recognized from the market, her grandson clutching her tattered sleeve. The boy couldn't have been more than seven, his eyes too large for his thin face, his small frame trembling despite the warm spring air. Beside them waited a young mother with twins, both children sharing a single worn blanket. An elderly man with the bent back of a former farmer leaned heavily on a walking stick carved from bamboo, his dignity intact despite his circumstances. A woman of middle years held the hand of a daughter whose eyes held the clouded look of blindness, whispering soft reassurances about the kindness of the monks. These weren't strangers to each other, but rather formed their own small community of survival, sharing information about which temples gave food, which officials might be sympathetic, which streets were safest to sleep on.

"Grandmother," the child whispered, "when will we eat?"

"Soon, little one," she replied, though her own voice wavered with uncertainty. "The holy monks will share what they can spare."

Daoji felt his stomach clench. Not from hunger, for he had eaten well that morning, but from the sudden understanding of what "what they can spare" truly meant. The temple's morning meal had included fresh vegetables, good rice, and even small portions of pickled radishes and sesame paste. Yet these people, some of whom had been waiting since dawn, would receive only the scraps that remained.

"Brother Daoji!" Wuxin's voice carried a note of irritation. "You must not keep Master Hui waiting."

But Daoji was no longer listening. He had turned back toward the storage room, where the abundance of food mocked the empty bowls beyond the walls. Barely considering the consequences, he began gathering items: a large sack of rice, dried vegetables, a jar of oil, and even some of the precious sesame paste and pickled delicacies that were reserved for special occasions.

"What are you doing?" Wuxin gasped, hurrying after him as Daoji strode toward the rear gate with his arms full. "That food is for the community! It must be properly portioned, properly distributed according to our rules!"

Daoji paused at the gate, the weight of the food heavy in his arms but somehow lighter than the weight he had carried in his heart moments before. "Brother Wuxin," he said in a low voice, "when did we decide that our rules were more important than their hunger?"

Before the senior administrator could respond, Daoji pushed open the gate and stepped into the midst of the waiting crowd. Their faces turned toward him with expressions of hope mixed with confusion. Monks didn't typically appear with armloads of food during the morning hours.

"Please," Daoji said, setting down the sacks and jars, "take what you need."

The silence that followed was broken only by the distant sound of temple bells calling the community to morning prayers. Then the old woman stepped forward, her hands scarred by labor reaching tentatively toward the rice.

"Holy monk," she whispered, "are you certain? This seems like more than scraps."

"Grandmother," Daoji replied, using the respectful address that honored her age and wisdom, "you have been waiting since dawn while we ate in comfort. How can that be right?"

As the crowd divided the food among themselves, their thankful voices mixing with children's laughter rang out, Daoji felt a hand grip his shoulder with considerable force.

"Brother Daoji." Master Hui's voice carried no anger, but it held a gravity that made several of the beggars look up nervously. "A word, if you please."

They walked in silence back through the temple grounds, past the meditation halls where other monks had begun their morning practice, past the gardens where vegetables grew in neat, orderly rows. It wasn't until they reached Hui's private quarters that the old master finally spoke.

Master Hui stood watching him for several minutes before settling beside him on the ground, his aged joints creaking as he assumed a comfortable position.

"Tell me, Daoji," he said gently, "what do you see when you look at those people outside our gates?"

Daoji glanced toward the window where the sounds of grateful voices still drifted over the temple walls. "I see suffering, Master. Pain that I want to help heal."

"Good," Master Hui nodded. "Then you are ready to understand the Buddha's first and most important teaching. The Four Noble Truths that illuminate all existence."

He gestured toward the window. "The First Truth is that life contains suffering. Those people know pain, hunger, fear. So do we all. The Buddha called this dukkha, the fundamental unsatisfactoriness that marks all existence. Not just physical pain, but the deeper ache of being separated from what we love, of wanting things to be different than they are."

Daoji felt something stir in his understanding as he absorbed these words.

"The Second Truth," Master Hui continued, "explains why we suffer. It comes from our attachments, our cravings, our endless wanting. What the Buddha called tanha. We suffer because we cling to things that must change, because we desire what we cannot have, because we fight against the natural flow of existence."

He looked directly at Daoji. "Even our attachment to helping others can become a source of suffering if we cannot accept the limits of what we can do."

"The Third Truth," Master Hui's voice grew gentler, "offers hope. What the Buddha called nirodha. Suffering can end. It is not eternal, not unavoidable. When we release our attachments, when we stop fighting against reality, when we find peace with what is, suffering loses its power over us."

Daoji felt something shift in his understanding, like a door opening in a room he hadn't known existed.

"And the Fourth Truth," Master Hui concluded, "shows us the way. What the Buddha called magga. The Noble Eightfold Path, the method by which we can end suffering, not just for ourselves but for all beings. Right Understanding, Right Intention, Right Speech, Right Action, Right Livelihood, Right Effort, Right Mindfulness, Right Concentration."

The old teacher was quiet for a moment, watching as Daoji processed this teaching. "The question, young brother, is not whether you should help those who suffer. The question is how your compassion serves the greater purpose of ending suffering in the world."

"But Master," Daoji said slowly, "if the goal is to end our own suffering by releasing attachment, why should we become attached to helping others? Isn't caring about their pain just another form of clinging?"

Master Hui smiled, the expression transforming his usually stern features. "An excellent question. One that shows you understand both the teaching and its complexity. What do you think the answer might be?"

Daoji looked toward the window where he could still hear distant voices. "Maybe," he said tentatively, "there's a difference between attachment that comes from wanting something for ourselves, and compassion that comes from understanding that all beings are connected?"

"Yes," Master Hui said, his voice carrying the approval of a teacher whose student had grasped something profound. "The Buddha's compassion was not attachment but understanding. He saw that the suffering of others and the suffering of self arise from the same source. To heal one is to heal all."

He rose slowly, brushing dust from his robes. "But remember, Daoji, true understanding requires both heart and mind. Compassion without wisdom becomes mere sentiment. Wisdom without compassion becomes mere coldness. The Buddha taught the middle way between extremes."

Daoji absorbed this teaching, but something in his heart still rebelled against the practical implications. "But Master," he said, his voice growing more urgent, "that little boy, his grandmother, they were starving. Not metaphorically starving, not spiritually starving, but actually starving. How can we speak of tomorrow's hunger while ignoring today's?"

Hui was quiet for a long moment, his fingers tracing the

prayer beads that hung from his belt. When he looked up, his eyes held something between disappointment and understanding.

"You have the heart of a bodhisattva, Brother Daoji, but the judgment of a child. "The heart alone drowns in others' pain. The mind alone turns away from it. Together, they find the path that truly serves." But now you also understand the Buddha's teaching about why we suffer and how suffering can end."

"Then show me the middle way between feeding the hungry and preserving our reserves," Daoji challenged, his tone sharper than he intended. "Show me how to balance their empty bowls against our full storage rooms."

"The middle way," Hui said with infinite patience, "is to work within the system to create lasting change, not to make grand gestures that solve nothing and potentially create greater problems."

"The Buddha himself faced this dilemma," Hui continued, his voice taking on the rhythm of a teacher sharing well-worn wisdom. "When he left his palace, he first tried extreme asceticism, nearly starving himself to death. Only when he accepted milk rice from a village girl did he discover the middle path. Neither luxury nor deprivation, but balance." He gestured toward the window where grateful voices still echoed. "Your impulse honors the Bodhisattva ideal, but understanding asks us to consider consequences. If we empty our stores today, what of the sick monk who will need medicine tomorrow? What of the traveling pilgrims who will arrive next week, trusting in our hospitality?"

But even as the words were spoken, Daoji knew that somewhere in the temple, Brother Wuxin was already tallying the loss to their stores, his abacus clicking with the rhythm of scarcity. Beyond the walls, he could still hear the voices of the crowd, the sound of gratitude and relief that Brother Wuxin's ledgers could never record.

Word of Daoji's morning generosity spread through the temple like ripples in a still pond. In the scriptorium, Brother Shi paused in his copying to whisper approvingly to his neighbor. In the gardens, novice monks debated quietly whether such actions represented true compassion or dangerous precedent. Brother Bai, who managed the temple's relations with local officials, worried aloud about what the magistrate might think if reports reached him of monks distributing food without proper oversight. But it was old Brother An, nearly eighty and bent with age, who voiced what many felt: "In forty years here, I've seen much charity given with careful calculation. Today I saw charity given with a full heart. Perhaps there's wisdom in both approaches."

That evening, as the temple bell tolled the hour for meditation, Daoji found himself not in the hall with his brothers, but back at the rear gate, where a few stragglers still lingered. Among them was the small boy from that morning, his grandmother nowhere to be seen.

"Little brother," Daoji called softly, "where is your grandmother?"

The child looked up with eyes that seemed far too old for his years. "She went to find work, holy monk. She said the food you gave us today means she can work longer without fainting. She might earn enough for us to eat tomorrow too."

The simple statement hit Daoji like a physical blow. This wasn't about grand gestures or systematic solutions. It was about one day leading to the next, about creating the possibility for hope instead of merely preserving the status quo.

Later that night, as the temple settled into its customary quiet, Daoji knelt in the main hall before the statue of Guanyin. The goddess's serene face seemed different in the moonlight, less distant, more knowing.

"What would you do?" he whispered to the carved figure. "How do you balance infinite compassion with finite resources?"

The answer came not in words but in understanding, a sudden clarity that made him smile despite the seriousness of his situation. The goddess of mercy didn't balance anything. She simply responded to need wherever she found it, trusting that compassion itself would create the resources necessary to sustain it.

Rising from his knees, Daoji felt a profound change, like a door opening onto a path he had never noticed before. The rules of the temple, the expectations of his brothers, and even the disappointed concern in Master Hui's eyes were all human constructions, barriers built by minds that believed in scarcity rather than abundance.

But what if abundance wasn't about having more than enough? What if it was about giving more than seemed possible and discovering that somehow, there was always more to give?

The question would follow him into sleep and wake with him at dawn, becoming the first crack in the foundation of conventional wisdom that would eventually earn him a very different kind of reputation: not as Brother Daoji the obedient novice, but as Ji Gong the Crazy Monk, whose understanding of the Buddha's teaching would prove far too large for any temple's walls to contain.

Chapter 4

The Beggar's Bowl

T he winter rains fell in sheets across Hangzhou's cobblestones, turning the streets into rivers of mud and misery. Brother Daoji pulled his straw hat lower over his eyes as he made his way through the market district, his begging bowl clutched against his chest. The morning's alms collection had been meager: a handful of rice grains from a noodle vendor, a few coins from an elderly woman who could barely spare them, and more pitying looks than actual charity.

As he approached the familiar cluster of makeshift shelters beneath the East Bridge, the silence struck him first. Usually, the sound of children's voices would greet him long before he reached the settlement where the city's most desperate had built their fragile homes from scraps of wood, torn cloth, and stubborn hope. Today, he heard nothing but the steady drumming of rain on whatever surfaces could provide shelter.

The settlement had grown over the past months. What had once housed perhaps a dozen families now sheltered nearly thirty, as word spread that this was a place where people looked after each other. Daoji had been coming here regularly, bringing what food he could spare and often staying to help with repairs or simply to listen to stories that the rest of the city preferred not to hear.

"Master Lin?" he called, addressing the unofficial leader of the community, a former scholar who had lost everything in a failed business venture and now survived by teaching letters to merchants' children for a few coins at a time.

A thin hand pushed aside a piece of canvas, and Lin's gaunt face appeared, his scholarly beard now wild and unkempt. The man who had once quoted poetry with elegant precision now spoke in whispers, his eyes heavy with exhaustion and something that might have been despair.

"Brother Daoji," he said, his voice barely audible above the rain. "You shouldn't have come. The fever… it started three days ago. We've lost seven already."

Daoji's heart sank as he absorbed the full meaning of those words. He had heard of how the plague sweep through the poor quarters before, claiming those whose bodies were already weakened by hunger and exposure. But knowing about disease and witnessing its devastation were vastly different experiences.

"How many are sick?" he asked, already pushing past Lin into the settlement.

"More than half," Lin replied, following him with unsteady steps. "The children first, as always. Little Meiling passed this morning. Her mother…" He couldn't finish the sentence.

The largest shelter was a marvel of desperate ingenuity: wooden planks salvaged from construction sites formed the walls, held together with rope and prayers. Canvas stolen from abandoned market stalls stretched overhead, sagging under pools of collected rainwater that dripped steadily onto the inhabitants below. The floor was packed earth covered with woven grass mats, some so worn they were more holes than weaving. Sheets of oiled paper created small private spaces for families, while clay pots and chipped bowls served as the community's entire collection of cookware. Everything smelled of damp earth, unwashed bodies, and the lingering smoke from cooking fires that had to be extinguished when the rains came.

The smell hit Daoji immediately as he entered the largest shelter: not just the odor of unwashed bodies and damp clothing, but the sweet, sickly scent of fever and approaching death. Fear crept up Daoji's spine as he breathed the settlement's stifling air. Every instinct screamed at him to flee before the invisible seeds of disease could take root in his own body. He thought of the temple's clean dormitories, the carefully prepared meals, the safety of walls that kept the world's dangers at bay. How easy it would be to offer a prayer, leave what food he could spare, and return to the security of monastic routine. But then he saw a small hand reach out from beneath a tattered blanket, searching for comfort that wasn't there, and knew that his own fear was a luxury these people couldn't afford. In the dim light filtering through gaps in the makeshift roof, he could make out perhaps twenty figures lying on mats of woven grass. Some shivered despite the blankets that covered them, others lay ominously still.

His eyes found Widow Su in the corner, kneeling beside a small form wrapped in a faded blue cloth. Her keening was so soft it might have been mistaken for the wind, but Daoji recognized the sound of a mother's grief from his nights walking through the city's darker districts. Su was a seamstress who had lost her husband to consumption the previous winter and now faced losing her only child to the sickness that thrived in the cramped, damp conditions of the settlement.

"Sister Su," Daoji said gently, kneeling beside her. The child's face was peaceful in death, looking more like sleep than the end of a young life that had known little but struggle.

She looked up at him with eyes that appeared to hold all the world's sorrow. "She asked for you, Brother," she whispered. "At the end, she kept asking for 'Brother Daoji who tells funny stories.' Do you remember? You made her laugh even when she was hungry, teaching her to count using pebbles and making up tales about brave sparrows."

The words struck Daoji like physical blows. How many times had he brought small portions of food to this community, congratulating himself on his compassion while returning to his warm, dry cell in the temple? How many times had he offered words of comfort while sleeping on a clean mat, his belly full of the temple's adequate meals?

He knelt there for a long moment, holding Su's grief-wracked form while questions churned through his mind. What good were his prayers if they couldn't ease a child's suffering? What value did his meditation have if it didn't lead to action that could prevent tragedies like this?

"Brother," came a weak voice from across the shelter. An old man named Feng, a former soldier who had lost his pension to corrupt officials, was trying to sit up on his mat. "My grandson... he's burning with fever. Could you... could you stay with him? He's frightened."

Daoji looked around the shelter, taking in the full scope of the crisis. Here was real suffering, immediate and urgent, requiring not philosophical contemplation but direct action.

The temple's rules about maintaining proper distance from worldly concerns suddenly seemed not just inadequate but actively harmful.

"Master Lin," he said, rising to his feet with a new sense of purpose, "what do you know about treating the sweating sickness?"

"Little enough," Lin admitted. "Cold cloths to bring down the temperature, liquids when they can keep them down, warmth when the chills come. But we have no clean cloth, barely any water except what we can catch from the rain, and no fuel for fires."

"The physician won't come," added a woman whose own daughter lay semiconscious nearby. "Says there's no point treating people who can't pay and will only get sick again in these conditions."

"And the magistrate?" Daoji asked, though he suspected he already knew the answer.

Lin's laugh was bitter as winter wind. "Magistrate Wang's solution is to burn the settlement and drive us from the city. Says we're a pestilence that threatens the decent folk."

Daoji felt restlessness moved through him like caged lightning as he absorbed the full implications of what he was hearing. These weren't just poor people suffering from an unfortunate disease; they were human beings whom society had systematically abandoned, left to die in conditions that guaranteed such tragedies would continue.

"I need to return to the temple," he said finally. "But I'll be back before evening."

"Brother," Lin called after him, "don't risk yourself. The illness... it spreads quickly in close quarters. You have your whole life ahead of you."

Daoji paused at the entrance to the shelter, rain beginning to soak through his robes as he looked back at the scene of suffering behind him. "Master Lin," he said quietly, "what kind of life would it be if I preserved it by turning away from this?"

The walk back to Lingyin Temple seemed longer than usual, each step weighted with the memory of Widow Su's grief and the sight of those fever-bright eyes staring at nothing. By the time he reached the temple gates, his mind was churning with plans, each more audacious than the last.

He found Master Hui in the scriptorium, copying texts by the light of an oil lamp. The elderly monk had become more than a teacher to Daoji over the past months; he was a spiritual father whose gentle guidance had helped shape the young man's understanding of Buddhist compassion.

"Daoji," Hui said, looking up from his careful calligraphy, "you look troubled. Was the alms collecting difficult today?"

"Master," Daoji said, water still dripping from his robes onto the polished floor, "there's disease in the settlement beneath the East Bridge. Seven dead already, more dying. I need access to the temple's medical supplies. And food. A great deal of food."

Hui set down his brush carefully, giving Daoji his full attention. In the months since the young man had joined their community, the old monk had watched him struggle with the tension between monastic discipline and his irrepressible urge to engage directly with the world's suffering.

"I see," Hui said thoughtfully. "And what do you propose to do with these supplies?"

"Set up a proper infirmary. Provide clean water, warm food, medicine for the fever. Stay with them until the crisis passes."

"Stay with them?" Hui's eyebrows rose slightly. "Brother, you understand the risks? Fever spreads quickly in close quarters, and you have no training in healing."

"I have hands that can carry water and prepare food," Daoji replied. "I have a voice that can offer comfort to the frightened. I have a heart that breaks when I see children die from conditions that could be prevented with basic care. Isn't that training enough?"

Hui was quiet for a long moment, studying the young monk's face. He saw there a determination that went beyond mere stubbornness, a compassion that refused to be contained by conventional wisdom.

"Brother Wuxin tells me you've been... irregular... in your distribution of temple resources lately," Hui said finally. "Taking more than your share for alms giving, staying out past the evening bell. The community is beginning to talk."

"Let them talk," Daoji said, he spoke with more heat than intended. "While they debate proper procedure, people are dying from neglect."

"And if you bring the disease back to the temple?" Hui asked gently. "If your charity kills the sixty monks who depend on this community for their survival?"

The question hung in the air like incense smoke, heavy with implications that Daoji had not fully considered. The temple's resources were limited, carefully managed to ensure the community's survival through lean seasons and difficult times. If disease spread through the monastery, it could destroy everything they had built.

But as he stood there, still carrying the scent of the settlement's desperation on his robes, Daoji realized that some questions couldn't be answered with pure logic.

"Master," he said quietly, "what good is our survival if we

survive by turning away from those who need us most? What kind of Buddhism preserves itself while Buddhists refuse to practice it?"

Hui studied his student's face for a long moment, seeing there something that reminded him of why he had become a monk himself, decades ago. Finally, he rose from his desk and walked to a cabinet where the temple kept its medical supplies.

"Take what you need," he said, beginning to gather herbs, clean cloth, and small jars of herbal remedies. "But take also this wisdom: if you're going to risk your life for others, make sure you do it effectively. Before your departure, I would be pleased to share my insights regarding fever management."

The next hour was spent in intensive instruction as Hui shared everything he knew about caring for the sick. How to prepare herbal teas that could bring down fever, how to keep patients hydrated when they couldn't keep food down, how to recognize the signs that distinguished dangerous illness from recoverable sickness.

"The fever-reducing tea requires equal parts willow bark and chrysanthemum petals," Hui explained, demonstrating the proper proportions. "Steep them in water that has boiled and cooled slightly - too hot destroys the healing properties. For those who cannot keep liquids down, try small spoonfuls of rice water with a pinch of ginger root. Watch their breathing carefully; if it becomes shallow and rapid, elevate their heads and chest. Above all, keep them clean: fever sweats carry away the body's poisons, but they must be washed away, not left to fester."

"Most importantly," Hui said as they finished gathering supplies, "remember that healing is as much about hope as medicine. People who believe they might recover often do.

People who lose hope often die regardless of treatment."

As the afternoon sun broke through the clouds for the first time in days, Daoji made his way back through the city with a cart borrowed from the temple's storehouse. Word had already begun to spread about his mission, and several people stopped him along the way.

"Brother," called a merchant who had often given him alms, "is it true you're going to tend the fever victims yourself?"

"Someone must," Daoji replied simply.

"But the risk... surely the temple has ordained healers for such work?"

Daoji paused, considering how to explain something he was only beginning to understand himself. "Friend, if we wait for the properly qualified person to appear, how many will die while we wait? Sometimes the most qualified person is simply the one who shows up."

When he reached the makeshift village, he found that word of his return had preceded him. Lin and several other residents who were still healthy had begun organizing the space, separating the sick from the healthy as much as their cramped quarters would allow.

"Brother," Lin said, his scholar's mind immediately grasping the significance of the supplies Daoji had brought, "this is more than the temple usually shares. Won't you face consequences?"

"I'll face consequences either way," Daoji replied, beginning to unload clean cloth and medicinal herbs. "The question is whether those consequences come from helping people or from failing to help them."

He set up his improvised infirmary in the largest shelter, using his knowledge from Hui's hurried instruction to begin treating the sickest patients first. The work was exhausting and often heartbreaking. For every person whose fever broke, another worsened. For every moment of hope when a child asked for water, there was a moment of despair when breathing became labored and eyes grew distant.

Widow Su became his most devoted assistant, her grief transformed into fierce determination to save others from her loss. "My Meiling would have wanted this," she said as they worked through the night, bathing fevered bodies and spooning broth into reluctant mouths. "She always said we should take care of each other."

By the third day, a pattern had begun to emerge. Those who received treatment early, who were kept clean and hydrated and warm, had a much better chance of recovery. Those who had been left to struggle alone often progressed beyond help before Daoji could reach them.

But something else was happening as well. Word of the monk who was risking his life to tend the city's most desperate residents spread through Hangzhou like ripples in a pond. People began appearing at the encampment: merchants bringing clean water, women offering to help with nursing, even children carrying small gifts of food or flowers for the patients.

Master Qian the cloth merchant was the first to arrive, his usually pristine robes muddied from hurrying through the rain-soaked streets. "My own daughter had fever last winter," he explained as he unloaded bolts of clean linen. "I can spare what a monk cannot." Behind him came Grandmother Wu, a baker's widow who brought not just bread but knowledge: "I nursed five children through the sweating sickness," she announced, rolling up her sleeves. "Someone teach me what this monk is doing so I can help properly." By evening, a steady stream of citizens had found their way to the settlement, each carrying something useful: fresh water in ceramic jugs, bundles of firewood, even a physician's apprentice who quietly appeared and began examining patients without speaking of payment.

"It's remarkable," Lin observed as they watched a silk merchant's wife carefully feeding soup to an old beggar. "A few days ago, these people would have crossed the street to avoid us. Now they're treating us like family."

Daoji, exhausted from three days of constant work but oddly energized by the community forming around their crisis, nodded thoughtfully. "Perhaps that's what they always were, and we just forgot. Perhaps it takes a crisis to remind us that we're all in this together."

On the fourth morning, Brother Wuxin arrived with two other monks, his face pale with something beyond disapproval. It was fear. "Brother Daoji," he said, anxiety tight in his voice, "the abbot has received reports. Citizens are talking about a monk who ministers to plague victims against all proper precaution. The magistrate has sent word asking whether our temple has sanctioned this... irregularity. Questions are being asked about our commitment to public order." He paused, glancing around at the makeshift infirmary with obvious distaste. "The abbot wishes to speak with you immediately. I fear the consequences may be... severe. There is talk of reassignment to a mountain hermitage, or worse - expulsion from the order entirely."

Daoji looked around at the patients he had been tending. Most were recovering now, their fevers broken and their strength returning. But several still needed constant care, and the community that had formed around the crisis was fragile, dependent on the hope his presence represented.

"Brother Wuxin," he said respectfully, "as you can see, my work here is not finished. Perhaps the abbot could…"

"The abbot's orders are not subject to negotiation," Wuxin interrupted. "You will come now."

It was Widow Su who stepped forward, her voice carrying clearly across the community. "Honored monks," she said, addressing Wuxin with all the dignity her humble circumstances could muster, "this brother has saved the lives of my neighbors, risked his own health for strangers, and shown us what it means to truly practice compassion. If your temple calls that worthy of punishment, then perhaps your temple needs to examine its own understanding of virtue."

Sounds of agreement rose from the assembled residents, both sick and healthy. These were people who had learned to expect little from the world's institutions, but they recognized genuine care when they encountered it.

Wuxin's face flushed with indignation. "You forget yourselves," he said sharply. "This monk has duties and obligations beyond your immediate needs."

"Yes," said an old man who had recovered from fever the previous day, "he has a duty to practice what he preaches. He has an obligation to live his beliefs rather than merely study them."

As Daoji gathered his few belongings and prepared to face whatever consequences awaited him, Widow Su caught his sleeve.

"Brother," she whispered, "Meiling came to me in a dream last night. She said to tell you that the Buddha sees everything, even when the temples close their eyes."

Walking back through the awakening city, flanked by his

disapproving brothers, Daoji felt that message sinking into his heart like a seed. The settlement behind him was no longer a place of despair but a community where people had learned to care for each other. Lives had been saved, not just from fever but from the deeper sickness of believing they were alone in the world.

Whatever judgment awaited him at the temple, he knew he had discovered something more valuable than institutional approval: he had learned what it felt like to live his beliefs completely, without reservation or compromise. The young merchant's son who had once worried about proper charity had become a monk who understood that sometimes the most proper thing to do was to ignore propriety entirely.

As the temple gates came into view, Daoji felt not fear but gratitude. Gratitude for the chance to serve, for the trust of desperate people, for the discovery that compassion was not an abstract virtue but a practical skill that could transform both giver and receiver.

The fever had been conquered, but the real healing was just beginning.

Chapter 5

The Abbot's Garden

The Abbot's private garden was a masterpiece of controlled nature, where every stone had been placed with deliberate intention and every branch pruned to achieve perfect harmony. Ancient pine trees twisted skyward in elegant spirals, their shadows falling across carefully arranged river stones that guided visitors along winding paths. It was here, among the carefully crafted representations of natural harmony, that Brother Daoji faced judgment for his practical acts of mercy.

Beneath the ancient pines, miniature landscapes unfolded in careful succession: a cluster of weathered stones symbolizing the Five Sacred Mountains, a small pond reflecting the sky like a mirror, and a single ancient ginkgo, now displaying the golden leaves that temple poets had celebrated each autumn for generations. The air carried the subtle fragrance of jasmine and the earthy scent of moss that grew only where the gardeners permitted it. Even the silence here was cultivated; positioned to provide tranquility while maintaining connection to the temple's rhythm. Every element spoke of humanity's desire to improve upon nature's randomness.

Abbot Yuan Kong sat in lotus position on a raised platform of polished wood, his silk robes the color of autumn leaves, his shaved head gleaming in the morning sun. At sixty-three, he had governed Lingyin Temple for twenty-seven years, transforming it from a modest monastery into one of the most respected religious institutions in the province. His face, carved by decades of meditation into an expression of serene authority, revealed nothing of his thoughts as Daoji approached.

Yuan Kong had not always been a man who measured compassion in ledger entries. In his youth, he too had questioned whether monastic discipline served enlightenment or merely preserved comfort. But three decades of leadership had taught him harsh lessons about the difference between individual heroism and institutional survival. He had seen temples fail when their generosity exceeded their means, watched communities of monks scatter when donations dried up and local officials withdrew their protection. His transformation of Lingyin Temple from struggling monastery to provincial powerhouse had required countless difficult decisions, each one moving him further from the idealistic young monk who had once distributed his own meals to hungry visitors.

Master Hui knelt to the abbot's right, his eyes fixed on the gravel patterns before him. Brother Wuxin occupied a cushion to the left, a scroll of accounts balanced on his lap like evidence in a trial.

Several senior monks formed a semicircle behind them. Brother An, the temple's eldest resident, watched with the sorrowful expression of someone who had seen too many promising novices lose their way. His neighbor, Brother Shi, shifted nervously, clearly uncomfortable with the proceedings but afraid to voice any opinion that might mark him as sympathetic to the accused.

Behind them, Brother Bai exchanged meaningful glances with Brother Jing. Both men who had quietly supported stricter discipline for months, viewing Daoji's actions as dangerous precedent that could destroy the careful balance they had worked years to maintain. Only young Brother Mei, barely past his own novice year, looked openly conflicted, his eyes moving between the abbot's stern authority and Daoji's quiet defiance.

"Brother Daoji," the abbot said, his voice carrying the quiet authority of mountain stone, "you present us with a dilemma."

Daoji knelt on the bare gravel, feeling the small stones press into his knees through his thin robes. His body ached from the sleepless night, and his hands still carried the scent of herbs and sickness, but his mind felt clearer than it had in months.

"Please speak freely, Venerable Abbot."

"Brother Wuxin has presented me with a detailed accounting of your... appropriations... from our stores over the past three months. Food, medicine, cloth, even our precious honey reserves. By his calculations, you have given away resources equivalent to feeding our entire community for nearly a week."

The senior administrator unrolled his scroll with obvious satisfaction, displaying columns of figures written in his meticulous hand. "Furthermore," Wuxin continued, "his unauthorized distribution has encouraged increasing numbers of beggars to gather at our gates. What was once a manageable morning crowd has become a daily mob that disrupts our meditation and interferes with the devotions of legitimate visitors."

Daoji listened without speaking, watching a small bird land on one of the carefully positioned stones. The creature seemed unaware that it was disturbing the garden's perfect composition, focused only on the business of finding food to survive another day.

"And yet," Abbot Yuan continued, raising a hand to silence Wuxin's litany of complaints, "Master Hui reports that your meditation practice has deepened considerably. Your understanding of the sutras shows remarkable insight. In the debates with visiting scholars, you have demonstrated wisdom that surpasses many monks twice your age."

This was unexpected. Daoji looked up to find the abbot studying him with the penetrating gaze of someone who could read souls like scripture.

"Tell me, Daoji, how do you reconcile these contradictions? How can one who shows such promise in contemplative practice simultaneously show such disregard for the discipline that makes such practice possible?"

The question unfurled like sacred smoke, rich with hidden layers. Daoji felt expectation pressing on him from every monk present. Some were hoping he would repent and return to proper behavior, while others were perhaps hoping he would damn himself further with additional defiance.

"Venerable Abbot," Daoji said finally, "may I ask you a question in return?"

Yuan's eyebrows rose slightly. In twenty-seven years of governing the temple, few novices had presumed to question him during their own disciplinary hearings. "You may."

"When you meditate on the Four Noble Truths, what do you see as the source of suffering?"

"Attachment," the abbot replied without hesitation. "Craving. The ego's refusal to accept the impermanent nature of existence."

"And when you walked through the city to reach this temple all those years ago, did you see suffering there?"

"Of course."

"The same suffering? The suffering of attachment and craving?"

Yuan nodded slowly, beginning to see where the young monk's questions were leading.

"Then with respect, Venerable Abbot, how can we treat suffering as a philosophical concept while ignoring its physical manifestations? If a mother watches her child die of fever because she cannot afford medicine, is her attachment to the child's life merely an illusion to be contemplated, or is it suffering to be relieved?"

Brother Wuxin shifted uncomfortably on his cushion. "The Buddha taught that all suffering arises from within. External conditions…"

"The Buddha also taught compassion," Daoji interrupted Wuxin, he spoke with such vehemence that several monks straightened in surprise. "He taught that the path to enlightenment includes helping all beings escape suffering. When did we decide that meant all beings except the ones outside our gates?"

"You speak of compassion," Abbot Yuan said calmly, "but compassion without wisdom is mere sentimentality. If we give away all our resources today, what do we have to give tomorrow? If we die of the plague we catch while tending the sick, who will carry on the dharma?"

Daoji looked around the garden, taking in its perfect beauty, its careful representation of natural harmony achieved through human control. When he spoke again, his voice was quieter but no less intense.

"Venerable Abbot, forgive me, but I think we have confused preserving the dharma with preserving ourselves. The dharma isn't a collection of scrolls to be protected in libraries, or a set of rituals to be performed in sanctuaries. The dharma is a living truth that dies when it's not practiced."

"And you believe you understand this truth better than masters who have studied for decades?" Master Hui asked, his voice pained.

"I believe," Daoji said, turning to face his teacher with eyes full of respect and sorrow, "that truth isn't something to be understood but something to be lived. And I believe that as long as we live it safely, we're not living it at all."

"The great Master Xuanzang traveled to India and faced countless dangers to bring the dharma to China," Abbot Yuan said, his voice carrying the weight of historical authority. "But he did not throw himself carelessly into every crisis he encountered along the way. He preserved himself because he understood that his greater mission required survival, not martyrdom." The abbot paused, studying Daoji's face. "The Lotus Sutra teaches us that the bodhisattva vows to save all beings, but it also teaches skillful means: choosing the most effective path rather than simply the most emotionally satisfying one. How do you answer this wisdom?"

Daoji felt centuries of accumulated Buddhist learning pressing against his simple conviction. The abbot's question deserved a thoughtful answer, but his heart knew only one truth. The silence that followed was broken only by the sound of wind through the pine branches and the distant chanting of novices at their lessons. Abbot Yuan sat motionless, his expression unreadable, while the assembled monks waited for judgment to fall.

Finally, the abbot spoke, his words measured and deliberate. "Brother Daoji, your passion for service is admirable, but your methods are unsustainable. A temple that cannot maintain itself cannot serve anyone. I am therefore transferring you to our hermitage in the mountains, where you will spend the next year in solitary contemplation. Perhaps isolation will help you find the balance between compassion and wisdom."

The sentence was not as harsh as it could have been. Exile rather than expulsion, but it stung nonetheless. The mountain hermitage was not merely isolation - it was a kind of spiritual death. There, among the peaks where snow fell eight months of the year, Daoji would live in a single stone cell. His only human contact would be the monk who delivered monthly supplies. No letters from the outside world, no news of whether Widow Su had survived the winter, no way to know if the community he had helped build would flourish or crumble in his absence. The hermitage had a way of breaking men who were unprepared for its silence, but it had also produced some of the temple's most enlightened masters. Which category he would join remained to be seen.

"Venerable Abbot," Daoji said, bowing low, "I accept your judgment. But may I make one request?"

"You may."

"Allow me to return to the settlement once more, to ensure the sick are stable before I depart. Some may still need medicine, and there are bodies that require proper burial."

Abbot Yuan studied him for a long moment. "Very well. But you will be accompanied by Brother Wuxin, and you will take nothing from our stores."

As the assembly began to disperse, Master Hui approached his former student. His elderly face was creased with worry and what might have been regret.

"Daoji," he said quietly, "in the mountains, you will have time to think. Use it wisely. Your heart is in the right place, but a heart without discipline can cause as much harm as good."

"Yes, Master," Daoji replied, though they both knew his year of exile would likely teach him lessons very different from what the temple intended.

That afternoon, as he walked through the encampment beneath the East Bridge with Brother Wuxin trailing behind him like a disapproving shadow, Daoji first attended to the duties he had promised the Abbot. Three patients still showed signs of lingering weakness, and he carefully checked their breathing and pulse, teaching their families how to continue the herbal treatments in his absence. "The willow bark tea, twice daily until the moon changes," he instructed an elderly man caring for his grandson. "And keep him warm. The body needs all its strength to finish healing."

The burial rites were more difficult. Two bodies awaited proper attention, wrapped in whatever cloth the community could spare. With Master Lin's help and Brother Wuxin's reluctant supervision, Daoji performed the simple ceremonies that would give dignity to lives the city had chosen to ignore. He spoke the traditional prayers, but his heart added words of his own: gratitude for their trust, sorrow for their suffering, hope that their deaths might teach others about the cost of indifference.

Only when this somber work was finished did he find the community waiting for him. As word of his departure spread through the makeshift village, a small crowd gathered despite Brother Wuxin's obvious discomfort...

Master Lin, now fully recovered from his exhaustion, placed a small scroll into Daoji's hands. "Poems," he explained quietly. "To remember us by." An elderly woman who had survived the fever brought a handful of dried herbs. "For your health in the mountains," she whispered. Even the children came, their small faces solemn with an understanding beyond their years. They had learned that good people sometimes had to go away, but they had also learned that such people left something behind that could never be taken away.

Daoji spotted Widow Su, a solitary presence at her daughter's grave. She had fashioned a small marker from a piece of broken pottery, on which someone had painted a simple lotus flower.

"She would have been proud," Su said without looking up as he approached. "Last night, watching you tend the sick, she would have said that's what monks are supposed to do."

"I'm being sent away," Daoji told her. "To the mountain range, for a year of contemplation."

Su finally looked up, her eyes full of tears and something fiercer. "Then contemplate this, Brother: some of us will be dead when you return. But some of us will be alive because of what you did. Which truth do you think the Buddha would value more?"

As he prepared to leave the settlement, the weight of his choices settled over Daoji. Not just his own freedom, but the stability these people had begun to depend on. How many would die next winter without his advocacy? How many would lose hope without his presence to remind them that someone cared? The guilt was almost overwhelming, yet beneath it lay something unshakable: the knowledge that he had chosen to live his beliefs rather than merely study them. Whether that choice had been wise or foolish, time would tell. But it had been authentic in a way that felt more important than wisdom.

As he walked back toward the temple for what might be his last night within its walls, Daoji carried her question with him like a prayer. In the distance, the mountain peaks where he would spend his exile rose against the sky like pointing fingers, beckoning him toward a solitude that might teach him truths no monastery could contain.

The bird he had watched in the abbot's garden was long gone, but somewhere in the city, other creatures were finding food, building nests, caring for their young without consulting ancient texts or waiting for institutional permission. Perhaps, Daoji thought, that was a dharma worth learning too.

Chapter 6

The Mountain's Teaching

The hermitage clung to the mountainside like a prayer carved in stone, three small buildings connected by wooden walkways that creaked in the wind. Here, two days' journey from Lingyin Temple, Brother Daoji found himself alone for the first time in his nineteen years of life. The silence pressed against his ears like deep water, so complete it had physical weight.

The first weeks of his exile passed in a haze of wounded pride and spiritual confusion. He had been sent here to learn humility, but instead found himself wrestling with questions that grew larger rather than smaller in the mountain's vast solitude. Was compassion truly possible without wisdom? Was his desire to help others merely spiritual arrogance disguised as virtue?

Each morning he rose before dawn to sit in meditation as the sun painted the eastern peaks in shades of gold and rose. The view from his cushion encompassed valleys that stretched toward the horizon like a rumpled silk tapestry, but the beauty felt hollow when there was no one to share it with. He had grown accustomed to the sounds of human need, the constant small challenges of community life that gave shape and purpose to each day.

Here, there was only silence and his own restless thoughts.

"Perhaps this is what I needed," he told himself as autumn settled over the mountains, painting the sparse trees in brilliant reds and yellows. "Perhaps I was becoming too attached to being needed, too dependent on the gratitude of others for my sense of worth."

He tried to embrace the traditional hermit's life: long hours of meditation, careful study of the texts he had brought with him, mindful attention to the simple tasks of survival. The hermitage had everything necessary for a contemplative existence. A spring provided clear water that tasted of mountain stone, a small garden offered vegetables that grew despite the thin soil and short growing season, meditation caves carved by previous hermits invited deep introspection, and the vast silence seemed perfect for encountering the true nature of mind.

But as the first snows began to dust the higher peaks, Daoji discovered that solitude had unexpected teachers.

It was the fox that changed everything.

November had brought bitter cold to the mountains, and Daoji was emerging from his morning meditation when he noticed tracks in the fresh snow outside his door. Not the neat prints of a healthy animal, but the dragging, uneven marks of something injured and desperate.

Following the trail around the side of the main building, he found the creature that had made them: a red fox, its fur dull and matted, lying in a patch of weak sunlight with the exhausted stillness that comes just before death. One of its hind legs was twisted at an unnatural angle, probably broken in a trap and healed badly, leaving it unable to hunt effectively.

The animal's ribs showed clearly through its sparse coat, and its breathing was shallow and labored. It looked up at Daoji. His gaze reflected no fear, only the resigned acceptance of a creature that had exhausted all hope of survival.

For a moment, the two beings simply regarded each other: the monk who had been sent to the mountain to learn detachment, and the wild thing that embodied the harsh realities from which detachment was supposed to provide freedom.

The rules of hermitage life were clear: no involvement with worldly concerns, no distractions from spiritual practice, no attachments to impermanent things. A truly dedicated monk would see the fox's suffering as merely another lesson in the inevitability of death and the importance of accepting what could not be changed.

Daoji knelt beside the dying animal and fed it rice from his own bowl.

"Don't tell the abbot," he whispered as the fox accepted the food with desperate hunger. "He already thinks I'm hopeless."

Within a week, the fox had recovered enough strength to drag itself to the hermitage door each morning, waiting with patient intelligence for the crazy monk who shared his breakfast with woodland creatures. Daoji named him Ziran, meaning "Natural," for the way he lived the mountain's own wild wisdom, moving through the world without the complications that human thinking brought to simple situations.

As winter tightened its grip on the peaks, other refugees from the harsh season began appearing. A family of sparrows, driven from their usual roosting places by a fierce storm, took shelter in the eaves of his meditation hall. An old badger, its burrow destroyed by an early avalanche, made its home beneath his sleeping quarters. Even a young deer, wounded by hunters and abandoned by its herd when it couldn't keep pace, stumbled into the hermitage clearing and refused to leave.

The hermitage became something unprecedented in its century-long history: a sanctuary not just for human contemplation, but for any creature that needed refuge from the mountain's harsh indifference.

"This is ridiculous," Daoji told himself one morning as he divided his rice porridge among six different species of hungry animals. The monthly supply deliveries from the temple barely lasted three weeks now that he was feeding so many mouths. He had learned to supplement their meals with pine nuts, dried berries, and other mountain fare, stretching each delivery until the next monk made the treacherous winter journey up the path. "I'm supposed to be learning detachment, not running a mountain inn for every stray creature in the province."

But even as he spoke the words, he felt more at peace than he had since arriving at the hermitage. The animals asked nothing of him except food and shelter, offered nothing in return except their simple presence. Yet somehow, their companionship taught him more about the nature of caring than months of solitary meditation had managed.

By December, the hermitage had developed its own rhythm. Dawn brought the feeding of his adopted family, followed by meditation in the cave where previous hermits had worn smooth depressions in the stone floor. The middle hours of the day were spent in study, copying texts by the light that streamed through the single window, or in the practical work of maintaining the buildings against winter's assault.

But it was the evenings that taught him the most.

As darkness settled over the mountain and temperatures plummeted toward depths that could kill an unprepared creature in hours, Daoji would sit by his small fire with Ziran curled beside him, the sparrows roosting in the warm air near the ceiling, and the deer lying in the doorway where it could watch for danger while staying close to safety.

In these moments, he began to understand something that all his formal instruction had somehow missed: compassion was not a feeling to be cultivated or a virtue to be practiced, but a natural response that arose spontaneously when the barriers between self and other dissolved.

"You know, old friend," he said to Ziran one evening as wind howled around the hermitage walls, "I think the temple taught me to think of compassion as something difficult, something that required great discipline and careful consideration. But watching you accept help when you needed it, seeing how naturally the sparrows share food with each other, observing how the deer stands guard while the badger sleeps... it seems like caring for each other is just what creatures do when they're not confused by too much thinking."

The fox regarded him with ancient, knowing eyes, then simply rested its head on its paws and went to sleep.

January brought the deepest cold Daoji had ever experienced. For three weeks, temperatures never rose above freezing even at midday, and the wind carried a bite that could numb exposed skin in minutes. His small supply of firewood dwindled faster than he had anticipated, and he found himself facing a choice: use the remaining fuel to keep himself warm, or share it with his animal companions who had no other source of heat.

He chose to share, and discovered that huddling together

for warmth created a comfort that no solitary fire could have provided.

It was during this period of harsh survival that Daoji had his first true glimpse of what the Buddha had actually been teaching. One night, as he sat in meditation while snow fell outside and his breath made small clouds in the frigid air, he suddenly understood that the "self" he had been trying to transcend wasn't an illusion to be escaped but a boundary to be expanded.

The suffering he felt when Ziran was in pain, the joy he experienced when the sparrows sang in the morning, the protective instinct that arose when he heard hunters in the distance; these weren't attachments to be overcome. They were expressions of a mercy that included all life within its embrace.

"The mistake," he realized as dawn broke over peaks that glittered like crystal in the winter sun, "is thinking that enlightenment means caring about nothing. Maybe it actually means caring about everything."

February brought a crisis that tested this new understanding. Ziran's old injury flared up again, probably aggravated by the constant cold and the stress of surviving on limited food. The fox could barely walk, and Daoji could see in his eyes the same resigned acceptance he had seen on that first morning months ago.

There was an herb that grew in the valley below, a plant used by mountain folk to treat inflammation and pain. Daoji had learned about it from conversations with the farmers who sometimes brought supplies to the hermitage in autumn. But the descent to find it would take a full day in conditions that could easily prove fatal, and hermits were not supposed to leave their retreat except in cases of dire emergency.

"It's just a fox," he told himself as he watched Ziran struggle to reach the water bowl. "One animal among thousands. Attachment to individual creatures is exactly the kind of thinking I'm supposed to overcome."

But when he closed his eyes to meditate, all he could see was the fox's patient trust, the way the animal had never once doubted that help would come. How was that different from any human's faith that compassion existed in the world? How was Ziran's suffering less real than any other being's simply because it couldn't be expressed in words?

By noon, Daoji was making his way down the treacherous mountain path, a woven basket slung over his shoulder and a growing certainty in his heart that he was finally learning what the Buddha had actually tried to teach.

The descent was more dangerous than he had anticipated. Snow had covered familiar landmarks, making the path difficult to follow, and the cold was so intense that he had to stop frequently to warm his hands lest he lose the ability to grip the rocky handholds that kept him from falling into the mist-shrouded valleys below.

But when he finally reached the lower slopes where the healing herb grew wild among the pine groves, Daoji felt a surge of joy that had nothing to do with his own survival and everything to do with the possibility of easing Ziran's pain.

It was while gathering the precious plants that he heard unexpected voices echoing through the valley: human voices raised in distress and argument.

Following the sound, he discovered a scene that brought all his months of mountain learning into sharp focus. A young woman knelt in a clearing beside a rough shelter, clutching a bundle to her chest while an official in silk robes gestured angrily above her.

"The tax must be paid," the official was saying, his voice carrying the authority of someone accustomed to obedience. "Your husband's debt doesn't disappear simply because he's dead."

"Please," the woman begged, "I have nothing left. The baby is sick, I haven't eaten in two days. How can I give what I don't have?"

"Then you'll give what you do have," the official replied, reaching for the bundle in her arms. "The child can be sold to cover part of the debt. Even a sickly child can fetch something. There are always buyers willing to take a chance."

A small crowd had gathered to watch this confrontation, but no one moved to intervene. These were mountain folk, farmers and woodcutters who had their own taxes to worry about, their own officials to appease. Getting involved in someone else's troubles was a luxury they couldn't afford.

Daoji felt time slow around him, the moment stretching like a bowstring drawn to its limit. He could walk away, return to his hermitage with the herb for Ziran, and continue his year of contemplation without involving himself in worldly affairs. That was what a proper hermit would do. It was what Abbot Yuan expected him to do.

Standing there in the cold mountain air, Daoji finally understood what his months of caring for wounded creatures had been teaching him. The herb for his fox companion lay in his basket, a mother's desperation filled his ears, and suddenly the lesson became clear.

Kindness wasn't something you practiced in isolation and then applied to the world. Such love was the recognition that there was no isolation, that the boundary between self and other was an illusion that dissolved the moment you truly paid attention to what was in front of you.

"How much does she owe?" he asked quietly, stepping into the circle.

The official turned, taking in Daoji's rough hermit robes and weather-beaten appearance with obvious disdain. "This is government business, monk. Move along."

"How much?" Daoji repeated, his voice carrying a new quality that made several people in the crowd look up with interest.

"Fifteen silver pieces," the official said impatiently. "More than a beggar monk could earn in a lifetime."

Daoji reached into his sleeve and withdrew a small object that danced with reflected light. It was a jade pendant that had been his father's, the only thing of value he had kept from his former life. He had carried it through his months at Lingyin Temple and up to the mountain hermitage, not from attachment but as a reminder of the life he had chosen to leave behind.

Now, standing in a mountain clearing with a desperate mother and a sick fox both depending on his choices, he finally understood what that reminder was supposed to teach him.

"Will this cover the debt?" he asked, holding out the pendant.

The official's eyes widened as he recognized the quality of the carving, the deep green color that marked imperial jade. The piece was worth many times the woman's debt.

"I… yes, this would more than cover it," he stammered.

"Then take it," Daoji said, pressing the pendant into the man's hands. "The debt is paid."

As the official departed with his precious payment and the

crowd began to disperse, the young mother looked up at Daoji with tears streaming down her face.

"Holy monk," she whispered, "I don't understand. Why would you help a stranger? You don't even know my name."

Daoji knelt beside her, gently touching the baby's fevered forehead. "Though clearly unwell, the child's eyes still held life, potential, and hope that reminded him of Ziran's trusting gaze. "He reached into his basket of freshly gathered herbs and carefully selected what he needed. "These are for the fever," he said, wrapping the herbs in a piece of cloth. "Steep them in hot water - not boiling, just hot - and give the baby small sips. The fever should break by morning."

"Sister," he said softly, "what is your name?"

"Lotus," she replied. "My name is Lotus."

"Well then, Sister Lotus, now we're not strangers anymore. And as for why... "He paused, thinking of Ziran waiting patiently at the hermitage, of all the creatures who had taught him that compassion wasn't a philosophy but a way of breathing. "Because helping each other is what makes us truly alive. Everything else is just decoration."

The walk back up the mountain took longer than usual, slowed by the dangerous conditions and his frequent stops to gather more medicinal herbs. These weren't just for Ziran, but for a small supply he was beginning to think might be useful when he returned to the world below.

As he climbed, he felt something fundamental shifting inside him, like a seed that had been waiting all winter suddenly splitting open in spring soil. For months, he had tried to learn detachment by withdrawing from the world. But withdrawal, he now understood, wasn't the same as wisdom. True detachment meant being free enough from your own concerns to respond to others' needs without calculation or reservation. It meant caring so deeply that you stopped caring about the consequences.

When he reached the hermitage, Ziran was lying in a patch of weak sunlight, his breathing labored but his eyes still alert. Daoji prepared a poultice from the healing herbs and gently applied it to the fox's injured leg, speaking softly as he worked.

"You know what, old friend? I think we've been going about this backwards. The temple taught me that compassion was something you felt after you achieved enlightenment. But maybe enlightenment is something that happens when you stop worrying about achieving it and start paying attention to who needs help."

That night, as he sat in meditation with Ziran curled beside him and the sounds of his other animal refugees settling into sleep around the hermitage, Daoji felt more like a monk than he ever had in the formal halls of Lingyin Temple.

Over the following days, the healing herbs worked their quiet magic. Ziran's limp gradually lessened, his appetite returned, and the dull pain that had clouded his eyes began to clear. By late February, the fox was moving with something approaching his natural grace, though he still chose to stay close to the hermitage and the monk who had saved his life.

March brought the first signs of spring to the lower elevations, though snow still covered the peaks above the hermitage. One morning, Daoji woke to find that Ziran had disappeared during the night, leaving only paw prints in the soft earth around the buildings.

For three days, he searched the surrounding area, calling the fox's name and leaving food at places where they had often sat together. But gradually, he came to understand that Ziran's departure was not abandonment but graduation. The fox was healed, strong enough to return to its wild life, no longer needing the sanctuary the hermitage had provided.

Daoji felt a mixture of loss and profound gratitude. Ziran had been his teacher in ways that no human instructor could have managed, showing him that compassion was not a burden to be carried but a joy to be discovered.

The other animals began leaving as well. Over the following weeks, the sparrows found new nesting sites as the weather warmed, the badger disappeared into the awakening forest, and even the deer bounded away one morning without looking back. By the end of March, the hermitage was as empty as it had been when Daoji first arrived.

But the silence felt different now. Not the hollow quiet of isolation, but the expectant stillness of someone who had learned to listen for the calls of others who might need help.

By April, with only three months remaining in his year-long exile, but Brother Daoji had learned everything the mountain had to teach him. He understood now that his restless energy wasn't a spiritual flaw to be corrected but a calling to be embraced. His desire to engage with the world's problems wasn't attachment but awakening. His inability to find peace in withdrawal wasn't a failure but a recognition that true peace could only be found in engagement.

On a morning when the air carried the scent of wildflowers from the valleys below and the sound of melting snow filled the mountain streams with music, Daoji made a decision that would scandalize the temple hierarchy and delight the common people of Hangzhou.

He would not wait for his exile to end. He would not serve out the remaining months of his sentence. He would not return to Lingyin Temple to seek permission or forgiveness. He would go directly back to the world where people needed help, carrying with him everything the mountain had taught him about the difference between withdrawal and wisdom, between detachment and disconnection.

As he packed his few belongings and prepared to descend the path that had brought him to the hermitage, Daoji felt no sadness at leaving this place of profound learning. The mountain would always be with him now, not as a memory but as a way of seeing that turned every encounter into an opportunity for compassion.

The sparrows he had watched that first morning were already building new nests in the valley below, their wings knowing no barriers save the sky itself. It was time for the monk who had learned to fly in the mountain's vast silence to discover what miracles became possible when that silence gave voice to love.

The trail down the mountain beckoned, stone and earth formed into invitation, leading toward a world where spring was awakening not just in the natural realm but in the hearts of people who had forgotten how to hope for better things.

Brother Daoji, who would soon be known as Ji Gong the Crazy Monk, began his descent with the confidence of someone who had finally learned the difference between solitude and loneliness, between detachment and love, between being a monk and being truly awake.

Chapter 7

The Tavern Teacher

T hree months had passed since Brother Daoji descended from the mountain hermitage, three months of wandering the roads between villages, helping where help was needed and learning that the world had no shortage of people who'd been forgotten by temples and officials alike. He had transformed from the polished novice who once worried about proper procedure into something entirely different: a monk who belonged to the road rather than any institution.

The Drunken Phoenix Tavern squatted like a comfortable toad at the intersection of three busy streets in Hangzhou's merchant quarter, its red lanterns swaying in the evening breeze and its doors thrown wide to welcome anyone with coins to spend and stories to tell. Inside, the air was thick with the scent of roasted pork, steamed fish, and the sweet smoke of burning incense from a small shrine to the kitchen god tucked behind the bar. The tiny altar held offerings of rice wine and sweet cakes, ensuring Zao Jun's blessing on both the food and the establishment's prosperity, for what tavern keeper could afford to anger the deity who reported each year to heaven about the household's virtue?

Conversations buzzed at every table; merchants haggling over silk prices, scholars debating poetry, laborers sharing bowls of noodles and complaining about their foremen. Serving girls wove between the tables with trays of wine cups and platters of dumplings, while in one corner an old man played a bamboo flute that barely competed with the din of human voices.

The establishment had never before welcomed a Buddhist monk as a customer, but then again, no one had ever encountered a monk quite like the one who pushed through the crowd on this humid summer evening.

Brother Daoji (though few would recognize him as such) wore robes that had seen better days, patched with scraps of cloth in a dozen different colors: blue silk from a grateful merchant's wife, brown hemp from a farmer whose ox he'd helped deliver. His hair hung past his shoulders now, held back with a piece of leather cord, and his beard had grown wild and untrimmed around a face weathered by sun and laughter. Most shocking of all, he carried himself with the easy confidence of someone who belonged wherever he chose to be, regardless of what others might think appropriate.

"Wine!" he called to the tavern keeper, settling onto a wooden stool at the crowded bar. "Your best rice wine, and don't stint on the portion!"

The tavern keeper hesitated. "Brother, about payment..." Daoji smiled and produced a small silver coin, part of the modest earnings from helping a merchant fix his broken cart wheel that morning. "Even wandering monks must eat, friend.

And sometimes what nourishes the spirit comes in unexpected forms."

The tavern keeper, a portly man named Dong who had served everyone from silk merchants to pickpockets, stared at the monk with undisguised amazement. "Brother, are you... are you certain? I mean, aren't there rules about such things?"

"Oh, there are rules about everything," Daoji replied cheerfully, accepting the clay cup that Dong filled with obvious reluctance. "Rules about what to eat, what to drink, when to sleep, how to sit, where to look, what to think. So many rules that some people forget why they became monks in the first place."

He raised the cup in a mock toast to the tavern at large. "To forgetting the rules that make us forget ourselves!"

The crowd that had gathered to watch this unprecedented spectacle exchanged uncertain glances. At a corner table, a group of merchants whispered among themselves, clearly debating whether this was scandalous entertainment or dangerous heresy. Near the window, a young scholar clutched his wine cup with white knuckles, obviously torn between fascination and horror.

"Brother," said a voice from the crowd, "surely the Buddha taught moderation in all things?"

Daoji turned toward the speaker, a middle-aged man in the simple clothes of a clerk or minor official. "Indeed he did, friend. But tell me, what's moderate about hoarding wisdom in temples while people outside the gates go hungry for understanding? What's moderate about preserving purity by avoiding the very people who most need compassion?"

He took a long drink of the wine, savoring it with obvious pleasure. "This rice wine, do you know how it's made?"

The clerk shook his head, along with most of the crowd that had now gathered around the unusual monk.

"First, you take perfectly good rice, rice that could feed a family for days. Then you let it rot. You encourage decay, fermentation, transformation into something that seems ruined." Daoji held up his cup, watching the amber liquid catch the lantern light. "But that apparent destruction creates something new, something that can bring joy, loosen tongues, help strangers become friends. The rice had to die to become wine."

He set down the cup and looked around the tavern, his gaze taking in each person individually, completely. "Perhaps the Buddha's teaching is like that rice. Maybe it has to ferment in the real world, undergo some necessary corruption, before it can become something that actually nourishes human hearts."

Dong found himself leaning forward despite his initial skepticism, the monk's words stirring something he hadn't felt since his own youth: a sense that wisdom might come from unexpected places.

An uncomfortable silence settled over the Phoenix. This wasn't the kind of religious discourse people expected from monks (certainly not from monks drinking wine in public houses).

It was broken by a sound that made everyone turn toward the door: the harsh weeping of someone in desperate grief.

A woman stumbled into the tavern, her clothes torn and muddy, her hair disheveled. She looked around wildly, her eyes bright with tears and something close to madness.

"Please," she gasped, addressing the room at large, "has anyone seen my son? He's eight years old, wearing a blue robe. He was playing by the river, and then... and then..."

The tavern keeper stepped forward with practiced kindness; he had seen many kinds of pain stumble through his doors over the years. "Calm yourself, sister. Tell us what happened."

"The current was so strong after yesterday's rain," she continued, her voice breaking. "He fell in, and the water carried him downstream. We've been searching all day, but it's getting dark, and if he's in the water somewhere, hurt and cold..."

She couldn't finish the sentence, overwhelmed by the images her imagination conjured.

Several men in the crowd began offering practical suggestions: where to search, whom to notify, how to organize a proper rescue effort. But Daoji rose from his stool and approached the woman with a different kind of attention entirely.

"Sister," he replied with patience, "what is your son's name?"

"Little Tiger," she whispered. "We call him Little Tiger because he's so brave, so fearless. But the river..."

"Little Tiger," Daoji repeated thoughtfully. "A good name for a survivor. Tell me, does he swim?"

"A little. His father taught him last summer before... before the bandits came." Fresh tears coursed down her cheeks.

Daoji nodded, then did something that shocked the Phoenix into complete silence: he took off his outer robe, revealing the simple hemp clothing beneath, and handed the robe to the woman.

"Wrap this around your shoulders," he said. "You're shivering, and you'll need your strength."

"But... but you're a monk. I can't take your robes."

"I'm a monk whether I'm wearing robes or rags," Daoji replied. "But you're a mother who needs warmth, and that matters more than what I'm wearing."

He turned to address the crowd. "Friends, this woman's son is somewhere in the dark, possibly hurt, certainly frightened. We can sit here debating theology and drinking wine, or we can help her find him. What do you think the Buddha would choose?"

For a heartbeat, nobody moved. Then the clerk stood, lantern in hand. "If that were my boy…" He didn't need to finish. The merchant followed, then the scholar, then others whose names nobody knew but whose humanity the monk had somehow awakened. They filed out into the night, strangers becoming searchers, because sometimes the distance between 'not my problem' and 'how can I help' is just one person willing to cross it first. Within minutes, the tavern had emptied as people spread out through the city with lanterns and torches, calling Little Tiger's name into the darkness.

Dong grabbed his own lantern from behind the bar, his earlier amazement transformed into respect for the strange monk who had turned his tavern into something he'd never seen before: a place where strangers became family.

Daoji himself headed directly for the river, following an intuition he couldn't explain. As he walked through the muddy streets, still wearing only his simple hemp underclothes, several people stared in amazement at the monk who had somehow convinced an entire tavern to abandon their evening pleasures for a stranger's crisis.

The search stretched through the dark hours. Groups split up to cover different sections of the river, calling the boy's name until their voices grew hoarse. False alarms sent hearts racing - a bundle of rags that looked like clothing, shadows that might have been a small figure. As the night grew colder, some began to fear the worst.

Daoji followed the river systematically, wading through shallows and checking every pile of debris. It was past midnight when he heard it - a faint cry from beneath the East Bridge. There, caught in a tangle of branches and refuse, was Little Tiger, exhausted but alive.

"Are you the crazy monk?" Little Tiger asked as Daoji waded into the shallow water to retrieve him. "The one who drinks wine?" He'd heard stories from other kids in the village.

"I'm a monk who does what seems necessary," Daoji replied, lifting the boy in his arms. "Are you the Little Tiger who's brave enough to hold onto the bridge posts all night?"

"I was scared," the boy admitted. "But I kept thinking my mama would be looking for me, so I had to stay alive."

By the time they returned to the drinking house, word had spread through half the city. Little Tiger was shivering despite the warm summer night, his lips still tinged blue from the cold water, but his eyes were bright and alert. His mother ran anxious hands over his arms and legs, checking for injuries, her lips moving in silent prayers of gratitude. Apart from scrapes on his palms from gripping the debris, and exhaustion that made him lean heavily against her, the boy seemed miraculously unharmed. The crowd that had reassembled offered congratulations, free drinks, and not a few amazed comments about the monk who had orchestrated the rescue.

As the celebration continued, quiet conversations began forming around the edges of the crowd. "That family will need help through winter," said the cloth merchant, already calculating what he could spare. The baker's wife approached Little Tiger's mother with promises of daily bread, while others spoke in hushed tones about finding work for a widow with a young child. What had begun as a rescue was becoming something larger: a neighborhood deciding that this family would not face their struggles alone.

"Brother," said the young scholar who had watched the evening's events with growing fascination, "I've never seen anything like this. You drank wine, gave away your robes, turned a tavern into a temple. How do you reconcile such actions with your vows?"

Daoji, now wearing a borrowed shirt that was too small for him and still damp from his river rescue, smiled as he accepted another cup of wine from Dong, who poured with the reverence of a man who had witnessed something that changed his understanding of what monks could be.

"Young brother," he said, "I think you're asking the wrong question. Don't ask how I reconcile my actions with my vows. Ask instead: what kind of vows would prohibit helping a mother find her child? What kind of purity is preserved by staying clean while others drown?"

He raised his cup again, this time in a genuine toast. "To Little Tiger, who teaches us that survival sometimes means holding on when the current wants to carry you away. And to his mother, who teaches us that love makes every stranger a potential rescuer."

As the crowd drank to his toast, Daoji felt clarity crystallized within him: a sense of rightness that had nothing to do with rules and everything to do with response. This was his path: not the careful contemplation of distant compassion, but the immediate, messy, wine-soaked engagement with human need wherever he found it.

As the tavern finally quieted and the last grateful toasts were drunk, someone asked him, "What should we call you when we tell this story?"

He looked around at the faces of people who felt like family. Little Tiger slept peacefully in his mother's arms. The rough borrowed clothes, despite not fitting properly, felt more true than temple robes ever had.

"Brother Daoji died in the mountains," he said quietly. "Whatever feels right for who I am now."

By morning, the story would be all over Hangzhou: the crazy monk who drank wine, gave away his robes, and somehow turned a tavern full of strangers into a family willing to search the dark waters for one lost child. And people would call him Ji Gong - Lord of Compassion - though he never asked for the title.

It was, people would say later, the first miracle of Ji Gong, though he would always insist that the only miracle was what happened when people stopped worrying about what was proper and started caring about what was necessary.

Chapter 8

The Magistrate's Pride

Three weeks after the tavern rescue, Magistrate Wang Jinshan sat in his ornate office reviewing reports that made his jaw clench with increasing frustration. Across his red sandalwood desk lay a dozen scrolls, each one detailing another incident involving the monk the common people had begun calling "Ji Gong," the Mad Saint.

"He convinced the grain merchant's wife to open her family's private stores to flood victims," his secretary, Liu Ming, read from the latest report. "Without payment. She claimed the monk's words made her realize that hoarding grain while people starved was 'bad for her karma.'"

Wang set down his jade-handled brush struggling to control his irritation. At forty-five, he had governed Hangzhou's western district for twelve years through careful application of proper order, appropriate hierarchy, and firm boundaries between social classes. His success had earned him recognition from the provincial governor, and he had reasonable hopes of advancement to a more prestigious posting within the year.

Wang's rise had been methodical, earned through competence rather than connections. The son of a minor tax collector, he had clawed his way up from clerking positions through sheer intellect and unwavering dedication to the imperial system. Where other officials enriched themselves through corruption, Wang had built his reputation on efficiency and fairness within the established order. He had eliminated the worst abuses of his predecessors, streamlined the tax collection process to reduce burden on honest merchants, and maintained civil peace through twelve years of floods, droughts, and the occasional bandit raid. His success had come from understanding that sustainable authority required the consent of the governed; but that consent depended on everyone accepting their proper place in society.

Then this ragged monk had appeared, turning Wang's orderly district into a circus of unprecedented charity and social disruption.

Wang walked to a cabinet and withdrew a thick ledger, its pages documenting his twelve-year tenure. Here was evidence of his success: merchant disputes resolved fairly, public works projects completed on time and under budget, crime rates that were the envy of neighboring districts. The new bridges that allowed farmers to bring goods to market more easily. The standardized weights and measures that prevented cheating. The mediation system that resolved conflicts between guilds without bloodshed. He had created prosperity through predictability, peace through proper procedure. Why couldn't people see that his 'rigid order' was what allowed their daily lives to function smoothly? The monk's chaos, however well-intentioned, threatened to undo a decade of careful progress.

"Continue," Wang said tersely.

"Two days ago, he organized the dock workers into providing free labor to rebuild the Deng family's burned warehouse. Yesterday, he somehow convinced Master Bo (the silk merchant who never gives charity to anyone) to forgive the debts of seventeen families. The man claims the monk 'showed him the difference between wealth and prosperity.'"

Wang stood and walked to his window, which offered a view of the busy street below. Even now, he could see the monk's influence at work: groups of people sharing food openly, merchants helping customers who couldn't afford full prices, children from different social classes playing together in ways that would have been unthinkable just weeks ago.

"The man is dangerous," Wang declared. "Not because he's criminal, but because he's undermining the very foundations of civilized society. Order depends on everyone knowing their place and staying in it. If servants start thinking they deserve the same treatment as their masters, if beggars begin expecting charity as a right rather than a privilege, if the poor stop accepting their lot with proper humility..."

Even as he spoke, Wang felt the familiar tightness in his chest that came when his public certainty warred with private doubt. Was he truly concerned about social stability, or was he protecting his own position? The question haunted his quiet moments, though he had learned to suppress it during daylight hours. He had seen corrupt officials justify their worst excesses as 'maintaining order,' and had promised himself he would never become one of them. Yet here he was, plotting against a monk whose only crime was excessive charity. The irony was not lost on him, though he pushed it from his mind with practiced ease.

He didn't finish the sentence, but Liu Ming understood.

Social chaos. The breakdown of the hierarchies that made governance possible. The end of the stable world that had elevated capable men like Wang Jinshan to positions of authority and comfort.

"Sir, what would you have me do? Technically, he's broken no laws. His actions are... irregular... but not illegal."

Wang turned back to his desk, his mind already formulating a plan. The truth Wang rarely admitted, even to himself, was that his fears ran deeper than career concerns. He had grown up hearing stories of the chaotic years when regional military commanders turned against imperial authority, carving up territories like butchers dividing meat. The old men spoke of what happened when social bonds dissolved: neighbor turning against neighbor, the strong preying on the weak without restraint, entire communities scattered like leaves before a storm. His rigid adherence to hierarchy wasn't just about maintaining his position - it was about preventing the return of those dark years when law meant nothing and might made right. The monk's philosophy, beautiful as it sounded, would lead inevitably to that same chaos. At least, that's what Wang told himself when he wondered whether his opposition to Ji Gong was righteousness or mere self-preservation. "Then we create an opportunity for him to break a law..."

That afternoon, Wang instructed his guards to bring him reports of any major disputes or crises in the district. He didn't have to wait long.

By evening, Liu Ming had returned with news of exactly the kind of situation Wang had hoped for.

"The Zhao family merchant house is in crisis," Liu Ming reported. "Master Zhao's son was taken three days ago while traveling to visit his uncle in Deqing village. Young Zhao had only two guards with him. The bandits killed one and left the other for dead. The surviving guard crawled three li before farmers found him and brought word back to the city."

Liu Ming unrolled a piece of rough cloth. "They sent this with the ransom demand - the boy's outer robe, torn and bloodied, though whether it's his blood or the guard's, we cannot say. The message demands five hundred silver pieces, delivered to the old watchtower on Moon Ridge within seven days. Master Zhao has already sold his best jade, dismissed half his servants, and borrowed against next year's silk contracts, but he can only raise perhaps three hundred pieces."

Wang smiled for the first time in weeks. "Perfect. Make sure word of this crisis reaches our charitable monk. Let's see how his philosophy of universal compassion fares against professional criminals."

At the Zhao compound, the family's ordeal had transformed the usually bustling merchant house into a tomb of whispered prayers and sleepless vigils. Master Zhao's wife, Mei Lin, had not eaten since word of the kidnapping arrived, spending her days burning incense before the household shrine and her nights walking the courtyard like a restless ghost. Their elder son had ridden out twice with search parties, returning mud-soaked and empty-handed, his usual arrogance replaced by hollow-eyed desperation.

The servants spoke in hushed tones, many offering their own meager savings toward the ransom. Auntie Chen, who had helped raise both Zhao boys, wept openly as she prepared meals no one would eat. Even the family's competitors sent messages of support - in the merchant community, the kidnapping of a son struck at every parent's deepest fear.

The news of young Zhao's kidnapping spread through the

district like spilled oil, carrying with it the family's desperate pleas for help. Master Zhao, a textile merchant known more for his shrewd business practices than his generosity, had been transformed overnight into a grieving father willing to pay any price for his son's return.

Ji Gong heard the news as he sat sharing dinner with a group of day laborers outside a noodle stall. The men had been describing the kidnapping with the mixture of sympathy and resignation of men who knew what hardship meant but lacked the power to help.

"It's a shame," said Mu the carpenter, slurping his soup thoughtfully. "The boy's only sixteen, never hurt anyone. But what can be done? The bandits know those mountain paths like their own courtyard, and they've got the boy hidden where no one will find him."

"The magistrate won't help?" Ji Gong asked, though he suspected he already knew the answer.

"Claims it's too dangerous, too expensive," replied Yu the stone-cutter. "Says the family should have been more careful, hired better guards. Easy enough to say when it's not your son."

Ji Gong set down his bowl, his mind already working through possibilities. "Tell me about these bandits. Do they always demand silver?"

"Always," Mu confirmed. "Old Tiger's gang. They've been working these mountains for years. They take merchants' children, hold them until the families pay, then disappear back into the caves. Never hurt the children, mind you, but they always collect their silver."

"And if the families can't pay?"

The men exchanged uncomfortable glances. "Well," Yu said

finally, "let's just say the bandits have other ways of making money from healthy young people."

After the laborers departed for their evening rest, Ji Gong lingered at Grandmother Pan's stall. The old woman had been listening to their conversation with the knowing expression of someone who had heard such stories before. She had fed workers and travelers for forty-two years, and her memory was better than any official record.

"Old Tiger's gang, you say?" she mused, ladling soup into his bowl. "Aye, I remember when he was Squad Leader Liang, before his fall. Good man then - used to stop here with his patrols, always paid fair price, never demanded soldier's discount like some. Shame what happened to him."

"What did happen?" Ji Gong asked gently.

"Politics," she spat. "New commander wanted his own people in charge. Accused Liang of selling army rice to civilians during the famine. Course, he was sharing it out: selling what he could at fair prices, giving away the rest - to keep families from starving when the relief shipments got 'delayed.' But that didn't matter to the new commander."

The next morning, Ji Gong made his way through the merchant quarter, listening to how news of the kidnapping spread through different levels of society. At the silk shop, wealthy customers whispered about hiring additional guards for their own families. In the tea houses, scholars debated whether the government's failure to protect trade routes indicated deeper imperial weakness.

But it was in the workers' district that Ji Gong found the most useful information. A former soldier named Captain Wu, now reduced to loading cargo at the docks, had served under Liang before his disgrace.

"Squad Leader was the best officer I served under," Wu said quietly, glancing around to make sure they weren't overheard. "Never asked us to do anything he wouldn't do himself. When supplies ran short, he ate last. When we took enemy prisoners, he made sure they were treated proper, even when his superiors wanted… harsher methods."

"What changed him into Old Tiger?" Ji Gong asked.

Wu's face darkened. "Betrayal changes a man. Makes him trust no one, believe in nothing. But underneath…" He shook his head. "Sometimes I wonder if Squad Leader Liang is still in there somewhere, just buried under years of bitterness."

Young Zhao Weiming was not the typical pampered merchant's son. At sixteen, he possessed a kindness that made him beloved by servants and customers alike, spending his childhood playing with the dock workers' sons rather than looking down on laborers.

"He wants to study the classics," Master Zhao had confided to friends, pride and worry warring in his voice. "Says understanding people is more important than understanding profit." It was this very compassion that had led the boy to travel with minimal guards, refusing to intimidate the country folk with an armed escort. Now that trusting nature might cost him his life."

That night, Ji Gong made his way through the narrow streets to the Zhao family compound. Before he had even entered the compound, he could hear Master Zhao's voice through the windows, sharp with an anger born of helplessness.

"Twenty-three years building this business! Twenty-three years of fair dealing, honest weights, paying my taxes on time! And for what? So bandits can steal my son and the magistrate can tell me it's too expensive to pursue justice?"

Inside the main hall, Zhao paced like a caged animal, his usually pristine merchant's robes wrinkled and stained. "I've spent my life believing that if you worked hard and followed the rules, the system would protect you. But the system protects itself, not the people who make it work."

When Ji Gong entered, Zhao turned toward him with eyes blazing with fury unlike anything the monk had seen. "You know what the worst part is, monk? I've spent sixteen years teaching my son to be better than I am. More generous, more trusting, kinder to those below his station. And now those very virtues may have killed him. What father teaches his child compassion in a world that rewards only cruelty?"

Settling into the richly appointed hall, Ji Gong listened as Zhao described the kidnapping in detail. The boy had been taken while traveling to visit relatives in a neighboring town. The bandits' ransom note had arrived the following morning, along with a piece of his torn outer robe as proof they held him.

"Five hundred silver pieces," Zhao said, his voice breaking. "It might as well be five thousand. I'm comfortable, but not wealthy enough for that kind of sum. I've sold everything I can, borrowed from every associate, but I can only raise perhaps half the amount."

"And the bandits' response to partial payment?"

"They refuse negotiation. Full amount, or..." Zhao couldn't finish the sentence.

Ji Gong sat quietly for a moment, studying the merchant's face. Here was a man who had spent his life calculating profit and loss, measuring every transaction in terms of advantage gained or lost. Yet now he faced a situation where all his accumulated skills meant nothing.

"Master Zhao," Ji Gong said finally, "what if I told you there was a way to save your son without paying the ransom?"

Hope flared in the merchant's eyes. "I would say name your price. Whatever you want, it's yours."

"I want nothing from you," Ji Gong replied. "But I want everything for you. Your son's safe return, yes, but also something more valuable: a chance to discover who you really are when everything you thought you were gets stripped away."

Ji Gong's eyes moved around the richly appointed room, taking in the signs of prosperity and careful taste. His gaze settled on a beautiful wine gourd displayed in a place of honor, crafted from polished wood and decorated with inlaid silver.

"Actually," he said thoughtfully, "there is one thing I would ask of you. That wine gourd - may I borrow it? Sometimes the most important conversations happen when strangers share something of value."

Master Zhao followed his gaze, understanding dawning in his eyes. "My grandfather's gourd? He always said the finest wine was meant to be shared with worthy companions." He retrieved it carefully, pressing it into Ji Gong's hands. "If you think it might help bring my son home..." He closed Ji Gong's fingers around the gourd. "Then consider it a gift, not a loan. Some things are more valuable when they're given away."

"It might help with more than that," Ji Gong replied with a smile.

Later that evening, after leaving the Zhao compound, Ji Gong sat in meditation at a small shrine outside the city, but his mind was not on emptiness. Instead, he considered the challenge before him like a weiqi master contemplating the placement of stones.

Force would not work - thirty bandits in a mountain

stronghold could not be overcome by one unarmed monk. Bribery was impossible - he had no wealth to offer. Official intervention had already been rejected. What remained was the one weapon Old Tiger would not expect: the truth about who he had been before bitterness consumed him.

The plan forming in Ji Gong's mind was dangerous not because it might fail, but because it might succeed. If Squad Leader Liang still lived within Old Tiger, if that man's honor could be awakened, then the consequences would ripple far beyond one kidnapped boy. A legendary bandit choosing redemption would shake the foundations of how people thought about justice, forgiveness, and the possibility of change."

The next morning, as Ji Gong prepared for the mountain journey, the enormity of his task settled over him like the burden of a thousand prayers. He was risking not just his own life, but the trust of all those in Hangzhou who had begun to believe in his approach to compassion. If he failed, if he was killed or forced to compromise with criminals, it would shatter the hope he had kindled in people like Dong and the families he had helped.

More troubling was the deeper risk: what if Old Tiger truly was beyond redemption? What if fifteen years of bitterness had killed Squad Leader Liang so completely that nothing remained but the brutal pragmatist who ruled through fear? Then Ji Gong would face a choice between his principles and his survival - exactly the kind of test that could destroy a man's faith in the power of compassion.

But as he shouldered his small pack and took up his walking stick, Ji Gong realized that this uncertainty was precisely why he had to go. Faith that avoided all risk was not faith at all, but mere comfort. True compassion meant extending hope even to those who seemed hopeless, trusting that some part of every person still yearned for something better than they had become.

When news of the monk's mission reached Magistrate Wang Jinshan, he smiled with grim satisfaction. "Excellent," he told Liu Ming. "By tomorrow night, we'll either have a dead monk and a valuable lesson about the limits of idealism, or we'll have a monk who's compromised himself by dealing with criminals. Either way, his influence over the common people will be finished."

Word of his mission had spread quickly through the district, dividing opinion between those who saw it as noble sacrifice and those who considered it foolish suicide. In the merchant quarter, opinions split along predictable lines. Established families with government connections whispered that encouraging such reckless heroics would only invite more bandit activity. "Mark my words," declared Master Tang the rice merchant, "this monk's grandstanding will bring Old Tiger's entire gang down from the mountains to raid our warehouses." But younger merchants, especially those who had struggled to establish themselves, spoke differently. "At least someone's willing to act when the authorities won't," muttered the cloth dyer, whose own shipments had been threatened by bandits the previous season.

Among the laborers and artisans, Ji Gong's mission was met with fierce approval. "Finally, someone who doesn't just preach about compassion but lives it," said carpenter Mu, whose opinion carried weight in the workers' district. But even supporters worried about the precedent. "What happens to the rest of us if our crazy monk gets himself killed?" asked

Widow Tan, who sold vegetables in the market. "Who'll speak for the poor then?"

Meanwhile Magistrate Wang had been busy throughout the day, working to ensure the monk's mission would fail. A trusted messenger had been dispatched to the mountain passes with orders for any imperial patrols: if they encountered the monk, they were to observe but not intervene until the situation resolved itself, one way or another. Wang also quietly spread word among the merchant class that private rescue efforts, however well-intentioned, only encouraged bandits to demand higher ransoms from future victims.

"Let the monk learn what real criminals are like," Wang confided to Liu Ming. "Either he'll be killed, solving our problem permanently, or he'll be forced to negotiate with murderers, destroying his reputation for moral purity. Either outcome serves our interests."

Ji Gong set out alone for the mountains, following the old stone road that had connected Hangzhou to the interior provinces since the Tang dynasty. The first few li took him through terraced hillsides where farmers tended crops of rice and vegetables, their irrigation channels creating a geometric pattern across the landscape. But as the road climbed higher, civilization gave way to wilder country: dense bamboo groves that whispered in the wind, precipitous cliffs where mountain mists gathered like ghostly armies, and narrow defiles where the echoes of a single footstep could be heard for half a li.

This was bandit country, where imperial authority grew thin and local strongmen made their own laws. The few travelers Ji Gong encountered, merchants with heavy guards, government couriers riding fast horses, occasionally a patrol of imperial soldiers, all eyed him with a mixture of curiosity and alarm.

What manner of fool walked these dangerous paths alone and unarmed? By afternoon, he had left even these occasional encounters behind, climbing into the true wilderness where Old Tiger's reputation ensured that only the desperate or the foolhardy dared venture.

The mountains received him with their timeless silence, and somewhere in their hidden valleys, a sixteen-year-old boy waited for rescue by a monk who had already decided that some kinds of wealth were worth more than silver.

Chapter 9

The Bandit's Bargain

The bandit camp clung to a rocky ledge halfway up the mountain like a collection of bird's nests, accessible only by a narrow path that could easily be defended by a single archer. Old Tiger had chosen the location well: below lay a sheer drop into mist-shrouded valleys, while above rose cliffs that would challenge even the most skilled climbers. It was here, in this natural fortress, that he had built his new life, operating for fifteen years without once being captured by imperial forces.

Ji Gong approached the camp openly, making no attempt at stealth or surprise. His walking stick tapped against the stone path in a steady rhythm that announced his presence long before he became visible to the sentries. When he finally rounded the last bend, he found three armed men waiting for him, their faces showing the mixture of suspicion and amusement that marked professional criminals confronting an apparent fool.

"Well, well," said the largest of the three, a scarred man whose missing left ear spoke of past violence. "Look what's wandered up our mountain. A monk, by the look of him, though a shabby one."

"I am Ji Gong," he said simply. "I've come about the Zhao boy."

The bandits exchanged glances. Word of the crazy monk had apparently reached even these remote heights, though not necessarily with favorable implications.

"Old Tiger don't usually receive visitors," said the second bandit, a thin man whose nervous energy suggested someone who lived on constant alertness. "Especially monks who make trouble for honest businessmen."

"I make trouble only for dishonest businessmen," Ji Gong replied cheerfully. "Are you telling me your business is dishonest?"

The third bandit, younger than the others but with eyes bright with an old man's cunning, laughed despite himself. "Brother, you've got brass, I'll give you that. Walking up here alone, making jokes with men who could toss you off this cliff without breaking stride."

"Could you?" Ji Gong asked with genuine curiosity. "I wonder. It seems to me that men who make their living from other people's fear might find it difficult to harm someone who isn't afraid."

Before any of the bandits could respond to this philosophical challenge, a voice called from deeper in the camp. "Bring him up, boys. I want to see this mad monk for myself."

The camp itself was more sophisticated than Ji Gong had expected: not just caves and lean-tos, but proper shelters built into the rock faces, cooking areas shielded from wind and rain; where iron pots hung over stone fire rings and oil-paper lanterns swayed from bamboo poles, even a small corral where horses grazed on mountain grass. Perhaps thirty men moved about their daily business, their equipment well-maintained and their bearing more professional soldier than desperate outlaw.

The bandit leader himself sat on a natural throne formed by wind-carved stone, his massive frame draped in furs and silk, a curved dao resting across his knees and bronze ornaments glinting from his belt that spoke of successful "business ventures." His face bore the weathered dignity of a man who had survived by his wits and will in an unforgiving world, his gray beard carefully braided and his eyes sharp as winter stars. But Ji Gong noticed something else: a tightness around those eyes, a way of holding his shoulders that spoke of a man constantly prepared for betrayal.

"So," he rumbled, with absolute authority, "you're the monk who's been turning Hangzhou upside down with charity and philosophy. Come to lecture me about the error of my ways, have you?"

"Actually," Ji Gong said, settling cross-legged on the ground as if he were in a temple rather than a bandit stronghold, "I've come to make you an offer."

Old Tiger's eyebrows rose. "An offer? Monk, do you understand the situation here? I have the merchant's son. His father pays my price, or the boy disappears forever. It's a simple business arrangement with no room for negotiation."

"Oh, I understand perfectly," Ji Gong replied. "You've built a successful enterprise based on fear, desperation, and the belief that some people's lives are worth more than others. It's actually quite impressive, in its way."

Several bandits shifted uncomfortably at this unexpected

praise, unsure whether they were being complimented or insulted.

"But here's what I find curious," Ji Gong continued. "You've created all this," (he gestured around the camp) "this organization, this brotherhood, this alternative society where men who couldn't find their place in the regular world have found purpose and prosperity. Yet you've based it entirely on taking from others rather than creating anything yourselves."

Old Tiger leaned forward, his eyes narrowing dangerously. "And what would you have us create, monk? Poetry? Pottery? We're not scholars or craftsmen. We're men the world threw away, who learned to throw back." His voice carried decades of accumulated bitterness. "Do you know what I was before this? Squad Leader Liang of the imperial army. Fifteen years of faithful service, wounded twice defending imperial convoys. Then a new commander arrived who wanted his own men in positions of authority. I was accused of stealing rations that I had distributed to starving civilians during the famine. They called it theft; I called it compassion."

He stood abruptly, his massive frame casting a shadow over Ji Gong. "You want to know about these men? Iron Wolf there was a blacksmith until the guild masters decided they didn't like his foreign blood and drove him out. Stone was a farmer until corrupt tax collectors took everything he owned. After that, he turned to the roads to survive, which is how the bounty ended up on his head. Gray Fox was a merchant's guard until he refused to look the other way while his master cheated widows."

The men he'd named nodded grimly, their faces hard with old injustices. Iron Wolf's jaw tightened, Stone spat into the dirt, and Gray Fox's hand unconsciously moved to an old scar on his neck.

"So spare me your talk of what we should create," Old Tiger continued, his voice rising. "The world below created us by destroying what we used to be. We simply returned the favor."

Ji Gong absorbed this without flinching, seeing now the depth of wounds that had driven these men to the mountains. "You're right," he said quietly. "The world wronged you. All of you. But tell me this when you take a merchant's son, when you demand ransom from a grieving father, are you fighting the people who wronged you? Or are you becoming them?"

"We survive," Old Tiger shot back. "That's more than the world wanted us to do."

"You do more than survive," Ji Gong observed. "Look at what you've accomplished here. Thirty men, living in harmony, sharing resources, protecting each other, following your guidance because they trust your judgment. You've created exactly the kind of community that villages and cities struggle to maintain."

The assembled bandits stirred restlessly. This was not the kind of conversation they were accustomed to having with visitors.

"Pretty words," Old Tiger said, though his tone had lost some of its edge. "But words don't put food on the table or silver in the strongbox. The world below sees us as vermin to be exterminated. We respond accordingly."

Ji Gong reached into his small cloth bundle and withdrew something that made several bandits step back in surprise: a wine gourd, beautifully crafted from polished wood and decorated with inlaid silver.

"May I offer you a drink?" he asked, holding the gourd toward Old Tiger. "I find that the best conversations happen when people share something."

Old Tiger studied the monk with new interest. "You carry wine? What kind of monk are you?"

"The kind who's discovered that the Buddha's teaching is large enough to include everything that brings people together in truth and compassion. Even wine, when it's shared with the right intention."

He poured two cups of clear rice wine, offering one to the bandit leader. "This came from a tavern in the city, where I learned that strangers can become family when they stop protecting themselves from each other."

Old Tiger accepted the cup but didn't drink. "And what does this have to do with the Zhao boy?"

"Everything," Ji Gong said, taking a sip of his own wine. "Master Zhao has spent his life accumulating wealth, believing it would protect him from the world's dangers. You've spent your life taking wealth, believing it would give you power over those dangers. Both of you have made the same mistake."

"Which is?"

"You've both forgotten that the only real wealth is what you can give away, and the only real power is what you use to help others find their strength."

Old Tiger finally tasted his wine, his expression thoughtful. "Philosophical arguments won't ransom the boy, monk."

"No," Ji Gong agreed, "but they might suggest a better solution. What if I told you there was a way to get more than five hundred silver pieces? What if there was a way to get something worth more than all the ransom gold you've ever collected?"

The bandit leader set down his cup, giving Ji Gong his complete attention. "I'm listening."

"Release the boy," Ji Gong said simply. "Bring him back to the city yourself, publicly, as a gesture of... let's call it community service. Accept the grateful thanks of his family and the amazement of the people. Then stay."

"Stay?"

"In the city. You and your men. Not as bandits, but as what you actually are: a brotherhood of capable men who know how to organize, lead, and protect. Hangzhou is growing, trade is expanding, and there's more honest work than there are honest men to do it. You could make more in a year of legitimate business than you've made in fifteen years of robbery."

The silence that followed was broken by harsh laughter from one of the bandits. Iron Wolf stepped forward. "Honest work?" he spat. "From the same people who drove us out in the first place? You think they'll welcome us with open arms? The guild masters who ruined me are still there," Iron Wolf continued, years of anger bleeding through his words.

"And the tax collectors who stole my farm," Stone added bitterly. "The magistrates who wouldn't hear our appeals. You want us to go back and pretend none of that happened?"

A chorus of angry voices rose from the assembled bandits, years of resentment spilling out.

"They'll arrest us the moment we show our faces!"

"We're wanted men! There are bounties on our heads!"

"Easy enough for a monk to talk about forgiveness you never lost everything to their corruption!"

Old Tiger raised his hand for silence, but Ji Gong could see the doubt that had crept into his eyes. "You see, monk? Even if I believed your fairy tale about redemption, my men have practical concerns. Half of them have prices on their heads. The other half have enemies who would see them dead."

"And what about you?" Ji Gong asked quietly. "What are your concerns?"

Old Tiger was silent for a long moment, staring into his wine cup. When he spoke, his voice was barely above a whisper. "My concern is that fifteen years ago, I believed in honor, duty, serving something greater than myself. I believed if you were loyal and did your job well, you'd be treated fairly." He looked up, his eyes holding a pain that made several of his men shift uncomfortably. "They destroyed that man so completely that sometimes I wonder if he ever existed. What makes you think there's anything left worth saving?"

Ji Gong stood and walked to the edge of the camp, looking out over the valleys below where the lights of Hangzhou twinkled in the gathering dusk.

"Old Tiger," he said without turning around, "you've spent fifteen years proving you're stronger than the world that rejected you. But strength built on bitterness is just another kind of prison. What if you spent the next fifteen proving you're better than the world that rejected you?"

When he turned back, he found the bandit leader staring at him with an expression unlike any his men had seen before: something between wonder and terror at a possibility too large to grasp.

"And if we refuse?" Old Tiger asked quietly. "If we keep the boy and demand our ransom as planned?"

Ji Gong smiled, and for the first time since entering the camp, his expression carried an edge that might have been dangerous. "Then I stay here with you until you change your mind. I share your meals, sleep in your caves, tell stories around your fires, and generally make such a nuisance of myself that you'll release the boy just to get rid of me."

Several bandits laughed despite themselves, but Old Tiger remained serious. "You would do that? Risk your life for a merchant's son you've never met?"

"I would do that for thirty men who've forgotten they were more than the world told them they were," Ji Gong replied. "The boy is just the excuse. You are the reason."

Old Tiger turned away abruptly, not wanting the monk to see how deeply those words had struck. Several of his men shifted uncomfortably, unused to seeing their unshakeable leader at a loss for words. For a moment, the only sound was the mountain wind whistling through the rocks. When he finally spoke, his voice was rougher than usual. "We'll discuss this further. Tonight, you share our fire."

That night, as Ji Gong shared the bandits' simple dinner of millet porridge and pickled vegetables, the conversation around the fire was unlike any the camp had heard in years. Instead of the usual talk of targets and strategies, the men found themselves discussing dreams they'd thought long buried.

"I had a forge once," Iron Wolf said quietly, staring into the flames. "Forged the best weapons in three districts. Took pride in my work." He looked up at Ji Gong. "But what's to stop the same guild masters from driving me out again?"

"What's to stop you from being better than they are?" Ji Gong replied. "What if this time, instead of working alone, you had comrades to stand with you?"

Stone shook his head. "It's not that simple, monk. I've got a bounty on my head for highway robbery. The magistrate himself signed the warrant."

"You mean Wang?" Ji Gong asked. "I know him. He's more interested in appearing effective than actually being effective. What if your crimes were overshadowed by your service to the community?"

Gray Fox, who had been silent all evening, finally spoke. "You talk about going back to the city like it's just a decision. But some of us... we've done things up here. Dark things. Killed men who tried to resist. You think the families of the dead will forgive us just because we return a merchant's boy?"

From the shadows at the edge of the firelight, young Zhao listened with the sharp attention of someone whose life hung in the balance of this conversation. At sixteen, he was old enough to understand that these weren't abstract philosophical debates but discussions of life and death, redemption and damnation. The monk's words stirred something in him he hadn't expected: not just hope for his own freedom, but genuine concern for these men who had become something other than his captors during his days in the camp.

The fire crackled in the sudden silence. This was the heart of it not just the practical obstacles, but the weight of blood and guilt that each man carried.

"No," Ji Gong said honestly. "Some won't forgive. Some will always see you as monsters. But others will see what you choose to become from this day forward. The question isn't whether everyone will accept your redemption. It's whether you can accept it yourself."

Old Tiger had been listening without speaking, but now he stood abruptly. "Enough," he said, his voice cutting through the philosophical discussion. "Gray Fox is right. We've all done things that can't be undone. I appreciate your offer, monk, but we're not heroes in some children's tale. We're killers and thieves, and no amount of pretty words changes that."

He turned to address his men. "Back to your posts. We have a ransom to collect."

As the bandits dispersed to their duties, Ji Gong remained by the dying fire. But he wasn't alone. Several men lingered in the shadows, clearly conflicted by the evening's conversation.

"Master," whispered one of the younger bandits, barely more than a boy, "what if the monk is right? What if there really is another way?"

"Shut your mouth, Crane," hissed an older man. "You want to end up dancing on a rope? We all know what happens to bandits who surrender."

"But what if we could make amends?" the boy persisted. "What if we could actually help people instead of hurting them?"

The argument that followed was conducted in fierce whispers, but Ji Gong could hear the cracks forming in the group's unity. These men had followed Old Tiger out of loyalty and necessity, but the dream of something better was beginning to take root.

The next morning brought an unexpected development. Ji Gong woke to find the camp in the midst of heated argument. About a third of the men, led by Iron Wolf and Stone, stood facing the others across the central fire pit. Old Tiger sat on his stone throne, his face dark with anger and what looked like fear.

"You've divided my men," Old Tiger accused as Ji Gong approached. "Half of them want to follow your mad scheme, the other half think they should be preparing for war with the imperial forces."

"I've offered them hope," Ji Gong replied. "I can't help what they do with it."

Iron Wolf stepped forward, his blacksmith's shoulders squared with determination. He had spent the night wrestling with an impossible choice: loyalty to the man who saved his life, or the chance to reclaim what he'd thought lost forever. Honest work at a forge, the ring of hammer on anvil, a life without constantly looking over his shoulder. "Old Tiger, I've followed you for eight years. You saved my life when the guild masters tried to have me killed. But this monk... he's offering us a second chance."

"He's offering you death!" snarled Viper, one of the most hardened bandits. "You think they'll let us walk away from years of robbery and murder? You think a few good deeds will wash away the blood on our hands?"

"Maybe not," said Stone with the straightforward manner of a man who dealt in facts rather than feelings. Despite all his time in this rocky refuge, he still carried himself like a man more comfortable with soil than stone, his broad frame built for long days in the fields rather than quick raids on mountain paths. "But what's the alternative? Spend the rest of our lives hiding in these mountains? Watch our numbers dwindle as the imperial forces get stronger? Die here like cornered animals?"

Young Crane, the boy who had spoken the night before, moved to stand with Iron Wolf. "I don't want to be a bandit anymore," he said, his voice shaking but determined. "I want to be something my mother could be proud of."

"Your mother's dead," Viper reminded him cruelly. "Killed by the same imperial soldiers you want to trust now."

"Which is exactly why I don't want to become the thing that killed her," Crane shot back.

The argument escalated, voices rising, hands moving to dao hilts and the curved handles of fighting knives. Ji Gong watched Old Tiger's face as the leader realized his carefully maintained authority was crumbling. These men had survived by absolute loyalty to his leadership. If that unity broke...

"Enough!" Old Tiger roared, standing from his throne. The camp fell silent. "Monk, you've brought chaos to my family. These men were united under my command. Now they're at each other's throats."

"They're thinking for themselves," Ji Gong observed. "Perhaps that frightens you more than imperial soldiers ever could."

Old Tiger's hand moved to his sword hilt. "You go too far."

"Do I? You've kept these men together by being the one who made all the hard choices. But what happens when the choice isn't hard? What happens when there's actually hope for something better?"

The bandit leader's eyes blazed with fury and something deeper. The terror of a man who had built his identity around being necessary to others' survival, now faced with the possibility that they might not need him anymore.

"Iron Wolf," Old Tiger said quietly, "you want to follow this monk's plan?"

"I do, chief."

"Then go. Take anyone who agrees with you. But you leave empty-handed. No weapons, no horses, no supplies. If you want to trust the mercy of the city, do it without our protection."

Iron Wolf's face went pale. "Chief, that's a death sentence. The road down is crawling with imperial patrols. Without weapons..."

"You said you trusted the monk's vision of redemption," Old Tiger replied coldly. "Let's see how much."

Ji Gong stepped forward. "If they go, I go with them."

"As their guide? Their protector?" Old Tiger laughed bitterly. "You're one man, monk. What can you do against a patrol of soldiers?"

"The same thing I did against thirty bandits," Ji Gong replied calmly. "Talk to them."

For a moment, the two men faced each other across a chasm of philosophy and experience. Then Stone spoke up.

"I'll go too. With or without weapons." He was joined by young Crane, then three more men, then two others.

In the end, eleven bandits chose to follow Ji Gong down the mountain. Nineteen, including Old Tiger, remained in the camp.

As the small group prepared to leave, Old Tiger sat alone by the cold ashes of the previous night's fire. The camp that had once buzzed with thirty voices now felt hollow, diminished. For the first time since his fall, he questioned whether the strength he had built on bitterness might actually be a weakness.

Old Tiger reached into the leather pouch at his belt and withdrew something he hadn't looked at in years: a small bronze seal, tarnished now but still bearing the imperial mark that had once authorized his commands. Squad Leader Liang's seal, carried through a dozen campaigns, witness to oaths of loyalty that seemed like another man's memories.

He turned it over in his weathered hands, feeling the significance of what it represented. Honor. Duty. The belief that serving something greater than yourself mattered. The world had taught him those were illusions, lies told to keep good men compliant while corrupt men prospered. But sitting here in the ruins of his certainty, he wondered: what if the world had been wrong? What if he had been wrong to let its betrayal poison everything he had once believed?

The seal caught a shaft of morning sunlight, gleaming for a

moment like hope itself.

Ji Gong approached him one final time.

"You're afraid," Ji Gong observed quietly.

"Of what?" Old Tiger responded defensively.

"That if you let yourself hope again, the world will destroy you again. Just like it did Squad Leader Liang. But look around you've already been destroyed. The question is: will you stay broken, or will you rebuild yourself into something the world can't break?"

Old Tiger was silent for a long moment. When he spoke, his voice carried a vulnerability his men had never heard. "What if I try to be that man again and discover he really is dead? What if there's nothing left but this?"

"Then you'll find out. But staying here, you'll never know if Squad Leader Liang could have survived what Old Tiger could not."

As Ji Gong turned to leave, Old Tiger called after him. "Monk. Those men who are leaving… they're not betraying me, are they?"

"No," Ji Gong replied. "They're honoring what you taught them about brotherhood by trying to extend it beyond these mountains. That's not betrayal. That's the greatest compliment a teacher can receive."

The descent began in tense silence, eleven former bandits and one monk making their way down treacherous rocky paths without weapons or horses. They hadn't gone two li before they encountered their first imperial patrol.

"Halt!" called the patrol leader, a young captain whose armor gleamed with the polish of recent promotion. "State your business on the mountain road."

Ji Gong stepped forward, his patched robes fluttering in

the mountain wind. "Captain, I am Ji Gong, a humble monk. These men are former bandits who have chosen to surrender themselves and seek redemption through service to the community they wronged."

The captain's hand moved to his sword. "Former bandits? You mean wanted criminals. Men, arrest them all."

"Wait," Ji Gong said, his voice carrying a quality that made the soldiers hesitate. "Captain, what's your name?"

"Captain Song Hu," the young officer replied, though he seemed surprised to find himself answering.

"Captain Song, you've been hunting these mountains for months, trying to break up Old Tiger's gang. Today, avoiding bloodshed or loss of life, half his force has chosen to surrender. Isn't that worth more than a few arrests?"

"They're criminals," Song insisted, but his voice lacked conviction.

"They were criminals," Ji Gong corrected. "Today they're citizens seeking to make amends. The question is: do you want to be remembered as the captain who captured eleven bandits, or the one who accepted the surrender of men brave enough to change their lives?"

Iron Wolf stepped forward, his hands empty and raised. "Captain, I am Iron Wolf, wanted for highway robbery and assault on imperial tax collectors. I surrender myself to your justice, but I ask for the chance to work off my crimes through service rather than pay for them with my life."

One by one, the other bandits stepped forward, stating their names and crimes, asking not for mercy but for the opportunity to earn redemption.

Captain Song looked from the surrendering bandits to the monk who had orchestrated this unprecedented moment.

Finally, he sheathed his sword.

"Very well," he said. "But you'll all be under strict guard until we reach the city. Any attempt to escape..."

"There will be no escape attempts," Ji Gong assured him. "These men are walking toward their future, not away from it."

As the group began their descent toward the city, a lone figure watched from the mountain camp above. Old Tiger stood at the edge of the cliff, seeing his former men walking freely down the path he had convinced himself was closed to him forever.

For the first time since his disgrace, Squad Leader Liang stirred within the bitter shell of Old Tiger. Not dead after all, but sleeping, waiting for someone to prove that honor could survive dishonor, that hope could outlast betrayal.

The boy, young Zhao, still sat in his simple prison, unaware that his fate was about to change forever. Because as Old Tiger watched those eleven men choose redemption over resignation, he felt his defenses beginning to crumble. Something that felt dangerously like hope.

"Viper," he called to his second-in-command. "Bring the boy. We're going down to the city."

"Chief?" Viper asked, confused. "What about the ransom?"

Old Tiger looked one last time at the path where Ji Gong and the surrendering bandits had disappeared. "There are some things worth more than silver," he said quietly. "I think it's time I remembered what they were."

Young Zhao walked among men who had once been his captors and were now his guardians, having witnessed the kind of transformation that changes not just lives, but the very possibility of what lives can become. The day when enemies became brothers, when bitterness chose hope, and when a crazy monk proved that the greatest transformations happen not through force, but through the simple recognition that everyone deserves a chance to become better than they've been.

The procession that would arrive at Hangzhou's gates would be unlike anything in the city's history: not eleven surrendering bandits, but thirty former outlaws walking openly toward redemption, led by a monk who had proven that even the most hardened hearts could choose hope over bitterness.

Chapter 10

The Return

Dawn broke over Hangzhou like a blessing, painting the rooftops gold and filling the streets with the gentle bustle of a city waking to ordinary miracles. These included merchants opening their stalls, children running to morning lessons, and grandmothers sweeping their doorsteps clean. But this particular morning would prove to be anything but ordinary.

The first person to spot the unusual procession approaching the city gates was Mu the carpenter, who had climbed onto his roof to repair loose tiles and found himself with an unexpected view of the main road. What he saw there made him call down to his wife with such excitement that she dropped her breakfast bowl and rushed outside to see for herself.

"Xiu Li!" he shouted. "Come quickly! It's… it's impossible, but it's happening!"

Down the dusty road came a sight that defied every assumption about how such stories were supposed to end. At the front walked Ji Gong, his patched robes somehow managing to look dignified in the morning light, his walking stick keeping rhythm with steps that seemed lighter than air. Beside him strode a massive figure in furs and silk: Old Tiger himself, his features marked by experience wearing an expression of determined uncertainty.

Behind them came the rest of the bandit gang, thirty men who had spent years avoiding cities now walking openly toward Hangzhou's gates. And in their midst, healthy and unharmed, walked young Zhao, his sixteen-year-old face bright with excitement rather than trauma.

"Is that...?" Xiu Li gasped, shading her eyes against the rising sun.

"The bandits," Mu confirmed, his voice filled with wonder. "All of them. Walking right up to the city like they're coming home from market."

Word spread through Hangzhou faster than fire through dry grass. By the time the procession reached the main square, hundreds of people had gathered. Some were drawn by curiosity, others by disbelief, and many by the hope that whatever miracle was unfolding might touch their own lives as well.

Magistrate Wang Jinshan arrived at the square in his official palanquin, his face a mask of barely controlled fury. This was not how the story was supposed to end. The monk should have been dead or discredited, the bandits should have remained safely in their mountains, and the social order should have reasserted itself through tragedy and failure.

"What is the meaning of this?" Wang demanded, stepping down from his palanquin with all the dignity his silk robes and jade ornaments could provide. "These men are wanted criminals! Guards, arrest them immediately!"

But Wang's personal guards hesitated, confused by the peaceful nature of the procession and the obvious cooperation of their supposed prisoners. It was Old Tiger himself who stepped forward to address the magistrate, his words booming across the square with authority of a man accustomed to command.

"Honored Magistrate," he said, offering a bow that was respectful without being servile, "we have come to return young Master Zhao to his family and to make restitution for our past... business practices."

Wang's eyes narrowed. "Restitution? Do you think you can simply apologize for fifteen years of robbery and kidnapping?"

"No," Old Tiger replied calmly. "I think we can spend the next fifteen years proving we're more than the worst things we've done."

From the crowd, Master Zhao pushed forward, his face tear-streaked but radiant with joy as he embraced his returned son. "My boy," he whispered, "are you hurt? Did they... were you treated well?"

"Father," young Zhao said, his words reaching every corner of the suddenly quiet square, "they shared their food with me, told me stories, taught me things about survival and brotherhood I never learned in school. When I was frightened, they comforted me. When I was homesick, they spoke of their own families. They are not what we thought they were."

Magistrate Wang felt the situation slipping away from him like water through cupped hands. "Nevertheless," he declared, "the law is clear. These men have committed crimes and must face justice."

It was Ji Gong who responded, stepping into the space between the magistrate and the bandits with the easy confidence of someone who belonged wherever compassion was needed.

"Indeed, honored Magistrate, justice must be served. But what form should that justice take? Punishment that changes nothing and helps no one? Or transformation that turns destroyers into builders, takers into givers?"

He gestured toward Old Tiger and his men. "These brothers have already begun their punishment. They've agreed to give up the only life they've known for fifteen years. They've chosen the hardest path possible: starting over, earning trust rather than demanding fear, building something instead of taking something."

"Pretty words," Wang snapped, "but society requires..."

"Society requires what serves society," Ji Gong interrupted. "Tell me, what serves Hangzhou better? Thirty men locked in prison, consuming resources and contributing nothing? Or thirty skilled, experienced men working to repair the damage they've caused while building new prosperity for everyone?"

The crowd stirred uneasily as people began to understand what was being proposed. These weren't abstract criminals being discussed, but men standing right there, flesh and blood beings who had chosen to walk down from their mountain fortress and place themselves at the mercy of the community they had wronged.

The square fell silent as a woman pushed through the crowd, her plain clothes marking her as someone from the working districts.

She carried a small child in her arms while two other children held hands beside her, the older one clinging to her worn skirt. When she reached the center of the square, she stopped directly in front of Old Tiger, her eyes blazing with a fury that made even the hardened bandit leader step back.

"You want to talk about restitution?" she said, her voice shattered the silence like a thrown stone. "You want to make amends for your 'business practices'?" Her voice broke on the last words, raw grief and anger finally finding their target.

"My husband was Jun, a guard in service to the Zhao family. Just days ago, he was escorting young Master Zhao through the mountain passes when your men attacked." She gestured toward her children, who clung to her with wide, frightened eyes. "These children will never see their father again. I don't even know how I'll feed them tomorrow, let alone next month."

The crowd erupted in hushed debate, some voices sympathetic to the widow, others uncertain about where this confrontation might lead. Old Tiger's face had gone pale, but he remained silent.

"So tell me," she continued, her voice rising with each word, "how is any of this right? How does walking down from your mountain fortress and asking for forgiveness bring back Jun? How does your redemption feed my children or comfort them when they cry for their papa?"

For a long moment, no one moved. Then Viper stepped forward, his weathered face etched with something between shame and resolution.

"What is your name?" he asked quietly, removing the leather cap from his head. "I would know the name of the woman I have wronged."

"Jingfei," she replied, her voice trembling with barely contained fury.

"Jingfei," he repeated, as if committing it to memory. "I was there that day. It was my blade that... it was me who killed Jun." His voice was barely above a whisper, but in the silence of the square, every word carried clearly. "He fought bravely, tried to protect the boy even when he was outnumbered. He died with honor."

Jingfei's face crumpled, fresh tears streaming down her cheeks. "His honor doesn't keep my children warm at night," she sobbed.

"No," Viper agreed, his own voice thick with emotion. "It doesn't. And nothing I can do will bring him back. But if you'll allow it, if you'll permit a killer to try to make amends, I vow before this entire community that I'll spend whatever years I have left ensuring you and your children never want for anything. My labor, my wages, my protection - everything I am belongs to your family until my dying breath."

Old Tiger stepped forward then, placing a massive hand on Viper's shoulder. "Brother," he said, his voice filled with the weight of leadership earned through years of hard choices, "what one of us has done to this community, all of us have done. Widow Jingfei, your husband died because of choices I made, orders I gave, a life I chose for all my men."

He turned to address his former bandits. "We came down this mountain together, and we'll face the consequences together. Widow Jingfei and her children are our responsibility - all of our responsibility. Whatever we earn, whatever we build, whatever prosperity we find in this new life, they share in it."

The other bandits nodded grimly, understanding that redemption came with a price that would last the rest of their lives.

Jingfei looked from Viper to Old Tiger to the other bandits, seeing in their faces not the monsters she had imagined, but men genuinely struggling with the weight of their past actions.

"You think promises can heal this wound?" she asked, but her voice had lost its edge of fury, replaced by exhausted grief.

"No," Old Tiger replied honestly. "But promises kept over years, over decades... maybe they can help us all learn to carry the weight of what can't be undone."

It was then that Master Bo stepped forward from the crowd. "Widow Jingfei," he said respectfully, "if these men are sincere in their commitment to your family, then they'll need work to make good on their promises. I have warehouse positions that need filling, and I'll ensure that a portion of their wages goes directly to your household."

Mu the carpenter nodded. "I'll need skilled help with the new bridge project. Any man working for me knows that caring for widows and their children is every citizen's duty."

"And I second that request," called Master Cao the rice merchant. "We need skilled workers in this city. We need men who know how to organize, how to lead, how to get things done. If they're willing to work honestly, then I'm willing to give them honest work."

Other voices joined in. Dong from the Drunken Phoenix needed help managing his increasingly busy establishment, the dock master required men to organize shipments, and the construction foreman could use experienced supervisors. Within minutes, tentative job offers were being called out from all corners of the square.

The responses from Old Tiger's men revealed the complexity beneath their unified decision. "Every day since leaving my forge, I've dreamed of working with honest tools again," Iron Wolf said to the gathering crowd, his scarred hands flexing unconsciously. "But I'll not lie: I'm afraid. Afraid my hands remember only violence, afraid the guilds will never accept a man with blood on his past."

Stone stepped forward. "Fear's natural. But staying afraid

in those mountains was just another kind of prison. At least down here, if we fail, we fail trying to be something better."

Young Crane, barely past twenty but already carrying the weight of hard choices, addressed the crowd with surprising eloquence. "Honored citizens, we know we don't deserve this chance. We know trust must be earned, not given. But we also know what it means to be brothers, to protect each other, to work together toward something larger than ourselves. If you'll teach us to turn those skills toward building instead of taking, we swear by whatever honor we have left that we'll not betray that trust."

Even Viper, who had chosen to remain with Old Tiger despite his doubts, spoke up. "I won't pretend this is easy for us. We've lived by different rules, harder rules. But a man gets tired of being only what the world expects him to be. Maybe it's time to find out what else we might become."

Magistrate Wang realized that his careful plan to discredit the troublesome monk had instead created a situation where he faced a choice between appearing compassionate or seeming petty in front of the entire district.

Yet here stood thirty men who had shattered those categories simply by choosing to walk down a mountain. Here was a community that had abandoned his careful hierarchies to embrace former enemies as potential neighbors. Here was chaos that somehow created more order than his regulations ever had.

"Liu Ming," he called to his secretary, who approached with obvious uncertainty about his master's mood. "Draft a report to the provincial governor. Tell him…" Wang paused, struggling with words that would reshape his own understanding as much as his superior's. "Tell him that we have successfully integrated a significant criminal organization into productive society through... innovative approaches to justice."

Liu Ming's eyebrows rose. "Shall I mention the monk's role, sir?"

Wang was quiet for a long moment, watching Ji Gong laugh with a group of former bandits and current citizens who seemed to have forgotten which was which. "Mention that local spiritual leadership played a... significant role in the rehabilitation process." Wang paused, then added, "Liu Ming, schedule meetings with the district's other magistrates . If this approach works here, perhaps... perhaps it could work elsewhere as well."

"Very well," he said finally, his voice tight with controlled displeasure. "Let it be recorded that these men will be granted probationary status. They will work under community supervision, make restitution through service, and face immediate imprisonment if they violate the trust being placed in them."

The cheer that went up from the crowd was spontaneous and joyful, people witnessed something they had never expected to see: enemies becoming neighbors, predators becoming protectors, a story ending in redemption rather than revenge.

As the crowd celebrated around him, Magistrate Wang felt the foundations of his worldview shifting like sand beneath his feet. He had built his career on the principle that order required clear categories: law-abiding citizens and criminals, those who deserved trust and those who didn't, stability maintained through predictable consequences.

The crowd's response revealed the complex social dynamics at play. Among the wealthy merchants, opinions split sharply. Master Tang the rice dealer whispered urgently to his associates about the danger of "rewarding criminality with opportunity," while his competitor, Master Cao, saw potential profit in men who understood logistics and weren't afraid of difficult work.

The artisans and shopkeepers showed more immediate acceptance. Blacksmith Yan approached Iron Wolf with professional curiosity. "I heard you worked iron before the mountains. I've been needing a partner who understands the craft, someone who can handle the complex orders while I manage the business side." The possibility of legitimate work in his old trade brought tears to Iron Wolf's eyes.

But it was among the laborers and servants that the bandits found their warmest welcome. These were people who understood desperation, who knew how easily circumstances could push someone beyond the boundaries of law. "We've all been hungry," said Widow Tan, whose vegetable stall barely kept her family fed. "We've all wondered what we might do if things got worse. At least these men are choosing to make things better."

As the crowd began to disperse and the bandits were surrounded by citizens offering work, housing, and tentative friendship, the practical work of transformation proved more complex than the emotional moment of acceptance. Master Bo the silk merchant approached Gray Fox with cautious optimism, but his questions revealed the depth of the challenge ahead. "Can you read?" he asked. "Do you understand contracts? My warehouse requires men who can track inventory, not just swing swords."

Gray Fox's face showed embarrassment. "Master. I know numbers, weights, measurements. Reading… that's been too long neglected. But I learn quick when I need to."

Similar conversations unfolded across the square. Stone

found himself explaining to a suspicious farmer how bandit organizational skills might translate to managing field workers. Young Crane was questioned by a merchant's wife about his willingness to live by city rules after years of mountain freedom. Each former outlaw faced the sobering reality that good intentions would need to be backed by practical adaptation.

Old Tiger approached Ji Gong with an expression of wondering gratitude.

"Monk," he said quietly, "I don't understand what you've done here. By all rights, we should be in chains or dead. Instead, we're being welcomed like returning heroes."

Ji Gong smiled, watching as one of the former bandits was already deep in conversation with a merchant about security work, while Stone was being led away by a farmer who needed help with his harvest.

"Old Tiger," he said, "you spent fifteen years teaching people to fear you. I spent but a moment teaching them to see you. The rest was just letting the truth have room to breathe."

Not everyone embraced the transformation with equal enthusiasm. Scholar Xu, who served as an advisor to several merchant families, voiced concerns that others shared but were reluctant to express. "This sets a dangerous precedent," he argued to anyone who would listen. "If we reward banditry with integration, what message does that send to law-abiding citizens who've struggled honestly for years?"

His concerns found echo among some of the older merchants. "What happens when they face their first real temptation?" asked Master Tang, whose warehouse had been raided by bandits two years earlier. "What happens when times get hard and old habits look easier than new ones?"

Even supporters acknowledged the risks. "We'll need safe-guards," admitted Master Zhao, despite his gratitude for his son's safe return. "Work supervision, community oversight, clear consequences for any backsliding. Trust is a gift, but it must be earned daily."

Captain Song, who had escorted the surrendering bandits to the city, offered a soldier's perspective: "These men know how to fight, how to organize, how to lead. That makes them valuable, but also dangerous. We'll need to channel those skills carefully, make sure they serve the community's needs rather than their own convenience."

Later that afternoon, as the excitement of the morning's events settled into the practical business of integrating thirty former outlaws into city life, Ji Gong found himself once again in the Drunken Phoenix Tavern. But this time, he wasn't alone. Half the establishment was filled with former bandits buying drinks for the citizens who had offered them work, their laughter mixing with that of their former victims in a harmony that should have been impossible.

Magistrate Wang, nursing a cup of wine in the corner and contemplating the complete failure of his plan to discredit the monk, watched the scene with a mixture of admiration and frustrated anger.

"How?" he asked when Ji Gong approached his table. "How do you make the impossible seem inevitable?"

Ji Gong settled onto the bench across from the magistrate, accepting a cup of wine from the jubilant tavern keeper. "Honored Magistrate," he said, "I think you're asking the wrong question again. Don't ask how I make the impossible seem inevitable. Ask instead: what if the things we call impossible are just the things we haven't tried yet?"

He raised his cup in a toast that drew in the entire tavern. "To Old Tiger and his brothers, who discovered that the greatest adventure isn't taking what you want, but giving what you have. And to Master Zhao, who learned that some treasures can only be found by letting them go."

As the tavern erupted in cheers and former enemies shared stories over shared wine, Magistrate Wang found himself facing an uncomfortable truth: the crazy monk's methods didn't just work; they worked better than anything established methods had to offer.

And that, he realized with growing unease, made Ji Gong the most dangerous man in Hangzhou.

Not because he broke the rules, but because he proved the rules were breaking everyone else.

Chapter 11

The Scholar's Test

The Imperial Academy of Hangzhou stood like a monument to learning at the heart of the scholarly district, its curved roofs and elegant courtyards designed to inspire contemplation and serious study. Within its halls, the finest minds in the province gathered to debate philosophy, compose poetry, and prepare for the examinations that could elevate a capable man to positions of influence throughout the empire.

Scholar Wen Zhiming had walked these marble corridors for thirty-three years, first as an eager student cramming classical texts into his young mind, then as an instructor molding other young minds in the same tradition. At forty-eight, his reputation extended far beyond Hangzhou's borders. His commentaries on Confucian administrative theory were quoted in the capital itself, his calligraphy graced the homes of governors and magistrates, and his poetry had been praised by men whose approval could make careers.

This morning, however, as he prepared for his advanced

seminar on bureaucratic harmony, Wen felt an unfamiliar unease settling in his chest like morning fog that refused to lift.

"Have you heard this name that everyone speaks?" his colleague Scholar Gao asked as they walked between the academy's marble pillars after the morning lecture on fiscal policy. The autumn air carried the scent of chrysanthemums from the carefully tended gardens, and the sound of students reciting classical texts drifted from the open windows above them. "Ji Gong, they call him. The common people speak of him constantly: a monk who performs miracles through wine and laughter."

Wen adjusted his scholar's cap with unconscious pride, the black silk and jade ornament marking his elevated status among the academy's faculty. "Miracles through wine?" He laughed, the sound carrying more derision than humor. "The common people will believe anything that relieves them of the responsibility for serious thought. No doubt this 'Ji Gong' is simply another charlatan taking advantage of peasant superstition."

"Perhaps," Gao said thoughtfully, pausing beside a stone bridge that arched gracefully over a stream stocked with golden carp. "But the stories are remarkable. They say he convinced an entire gang of bandits to become honest laborers. They say he can make enemies into friends with a single conversation. They say he has transformed entire districts through nothing more than compassion and common sense."

"They say many things," Wen replied, watching students practice calligraphy in the courtyard: beautiful, precise, endlessly repeating the same classical forms their masters had perfected centuries ago. "The masses always prefer entertaining fiction to difficult truth. Real wisdom requires years of study, disciplined thought, careful analysis of the ancient texts. It cannot be dispensed in taverns to drunken laborers."

But even as he spoke these words with his customary authority, Scholar Wen felt that strange unease deepen. Why was he being so vehement about a monk he'd never met? Why did the very idea of wisdom existing outside academic halls make his chest tighten with something that felt uncomfortably like fear?

That evening, instead of returning to his comfortable chambers to work on his latest commentary on the theoretical foundations of virtuous governance, Wen found himself walking through the common districts of the city. He told himself it was mere scholarly curiosity, a desire to observe the raw material from which proper society was constructed. But as he moved through streets he rarely visited, listening to conversations he rarely heard, something began to shift in his carefully ordered worldview.

The market was closing for the day, vendors packing their remaining goods while customers hurried to complete final purchases. The air was thick with the scents of cooking oil, dried fish, and humanity in all its unwashed vitality. Here, amid the press of bodies and babel of voices, Wen heard things that no classical text had prepared him for.

"Master Ji helped my family when the tax collectors came," said Widow Tan selling vegetables, her weathered hands arranging turnips with the same care Wen used to arrange his scrolls. "Not with silver (he had none) but with words that made the collector remember his own mother's struggles. The man left without taking anything, said he would speak to his superiors about adjusting our assessment."

Wen paused, pretending to examine some inferior calligraphy brushes while straining to hear more. Tax collection was a subject he'd written extensively about, but always from the perspective of administrative efficiency and revenue optimization. He'd never considered what it felt like to be on the receiving end of such policies.

"He taught my son that learning comes from watching as well as reading," added an elderly man mending fishing nets with swift, sure movements. "Now the boy sees lessons everywhere: in the flight of birds, the flow of water, the way strangers help each other. His schoolmaster says the child asks better questions than students twice his age."

This struck Wen more deeply than he cared to admit. He had spent decades teaching students to find the right answers in classical texts, but when had he last encouraged anyone to ask new questions?

"Most remarkable of all," said a young merchant closing his stall for the evening, his voice carrying the wondering tone of someone still amazed by his own transformation, "he makes you want to be better than you thought you could be. Not through shame or fear, but through hope, I suppose. He has a way of seeing the person you might become, and somehow that vision becomes more real than the person you've always been."

Wen felt his carefully constructed understanding suddenly invert itself, like a scholar realizing that all his years of copying texts had taught him to read the words but miss their meaning. These weren't the words of people deceived by a clever trickster. They spoke with the quiet conviction of students describing a teacher who had changed their understanding of the world. More disturbing still, they spoke of wisdom being applied to immediate, practical problems with results that any administrator would envy.

The courage that had been building in his chest finally overcame his scholarly reserve. "Forgive me," he said to Widow Tan, his voice carefully respectful, "but where might one find this Master Ji? I confess myself... curious about his methods."

Widow Tan studied him with eyes that had seen enough of life to read character in a glance. "You're from the academy, aren't you?" Her tone wasn't unkind, but neither was it impressed by his fine robes and careful speech.

"I am," Wen admitted, feeling strangely vulnerable under her direct gaze. "But perhaps... perhaps I'm beginning to wonder if wisdom might live in other places as well."

The widow's expression softened slightly. "Honest words, at least. You'll find him at the Drunken Phoenix most evenings. But scholar," she added with a knowing smile, "don't go expecting to stay comfortable. Master Ji has a way of showing people truths they didn't know they needed to see."

Walking through the evening streets toward the Drunken Phoenix, Wen found himself questioning assumptions he'd held for so long they'd become invisible. When had he last helped someone solve an actual problem? When had his learning touched a life in any way that mattered beyond academic advancement?

The Drunken Phoenix was busier than usual when he arrived, its red lanterns swaying in the autumn breeze and its doors thrown wide to welcome the evening crowd. Wen paused at the threshold, his scholar's robes marking him as clearly out of place among the laborers, merchants, and common folk who filled the establishment.

The contrast with his familiar academic environment was

jarring. Instead of hushed scholarly debates and the rustle of silk robes, he heard raucous laughter, animated discussions in dialects his education had taught him to consider "vulgar," and the clink of clay cups filled with wine rather than the delicate porcelain used for tea ceremonies in faculty meetings.

He found Ji Gong at a corner table, but the scene was not what Wen had expected. Instead of a charlatan holding court over drunken admirers, he saw a modest gathering of people engaged in what appeared to be a serious discussion about the nature of happiness. The monk's companions were an odd assortment: two former bandits who were now working as dock laborers, a silk merchant's wife whose expensive clothes contrasted sharply with her humble demeanor, an elderly beggar whose dignity transcended his ragged appearance, and a young girl who couldn't have been more than ten years old.

"Happiness," the little girl was saying with the gravity that only children can bring to important topics, "is when my grandmother smiles. She doesn't smile very often because her back hurts and we don't have much rice. But when Master Ji brought us medicine for her back, she smiled for three whole days."

"Ah," said one of the former bandits, a scarred man whose gentle voice contradicted his fearsome appearance, "but what about the happiness of accomplishment? Yesterday I helped build a new warehouse, and when it was finished, I felt something I'd never felt in all my years of taking things from others: pride in creating something useful."

"Both kinds of happiness are real," Ji Gong said, sipping his wine thoughtfully. "But I wonder: which kind lasts longer? The happiness of receiving something, or the happiness of giving something?"

Wen stood transfixed, watching this unlikely assembly discuss philosophical concepts with more genuine insight than he typically encountered in faculty meetings. There was no pretense here, no competition to display superior knowledge or elegant phrasing. These people were exploring ideas because the ideas mattered to their lives, not because understanding them would advance their careers.

It was then that Ji Gong noticed him standing uncertainly at the edge of their group, his fine robes and scholar's cap marking him as a visitor from a very different world.

"Master Scholar," Ji Gong said with genuine warmth, "please, join us. We're having a most enlightening discussion about the philosophy of contentment."

Wen hesitated. Everything in his training told him that serious philosophical discourse required formal settings, proper protocols, and appropriately qualified participants. The very idea of discussing profound concepts in a tavern with laborers and beggars violated every assumption about how wisdom was properly transmitted.

Yet something in the monk's voice (a quality of attention that pierced through pretense to reach whatever lay beneath) compelled him to accept the invitation.

"I confess," Wen said as he settled onto the rough wooden bench, his silk robes rustling against the crude furniture, "I'm not certain philosophy should be discussed in such… informal settings."

"Ah," Ji Gong replied with a smile that somehow managed to be both respectful and mischievous, "and where should philosophy be discussed? In halls where only the educated can enter? In books that only the literate can read? Tell me, Master Scholar, what good is wisdom that cannot survive outside a library?"

The challenge was politely delivered but unmistakable. Wen felt his scholarly pride bristle. He had debated the finest minds in the province and held his own against philosophers whose reputations spanned the empire. But before he could formulate a properly devastating response, the little girl piped up with devastating innocence.

"Are you really a scholar? Do you know everything?"

"Not everything," Wen replied, his irritation melting before her genuine curiosity. "But I have studied the great texts, the accumulated wisdom of our ancestors."

"That's wonderful," she said seriously, her young face bright with the hope that knowledge might solve problems. "Can you teach me something that would help my grandmother's back hurt less?"

The question struck Wen like a physical blow. Here was a child asking for the most practical application of learning (knowledge that could relieve suffering) and he had no answer. His years of study had prepared him to discuss the theoretical nature of virtue, the proper relationship between ruler and subject, the ideal structure of bureaucratic hierarchy. But when faced with a grandmother's pain, all his learning seemed suddenly irrelevant.

"I..." he began, then stopped, understanding dawning like sunrise over mountain peaks. All his knowledge was about abstractions (virtue, justice, order) but none of it connected to the immediate reality of human need.

It was Ji Gong who answered the girl. "Little Flower," he said with quiet conviction, "sometimes the best medicine isn't what we know, but what we do. Would it help if some of us visited your grandmother regularly? Brought her small gifts, helped with heavy work, showed her that she's not forgotten?"

"Oh yes," Little Flower said, her face lighting up with hope. "She gets lonely, and loneliness makes everything hurt worse."

"Then that's what we'll do," said the silk merchant's wife, a woman whose expensive clothes couldn't disguise the genuine compassion in her voice. "I have a cart, and these strong fellows can help carry whatever she needs."

As the group made practical plans to help one old woman's suffering, Scholar Wen sat in stunned silence. In just a few minutes, these "uneducated" people had demonstrated more useful philosophy than he typically encountered in a month of academic debates. They had identified a problem, developed a solution, and committed to action, all without consulting a single classical text or debating theoretical frameworks.

"Master Scholar," Ji Gong said quietly, his voice cutting through Wen's churning thoughts, "you look troubled. What are you thinking?"

Wen stared into his wine cup, seeing his reflection distorted in the amber liquid. The face looking back at him seemed like a stranger: a man who had spent decades accumulating knowledge he couldn't use to help anyone beyond his own career advancement.

"I'm thinking," he said slowly, each word carrying the weight of his worldview crumbling around him, "that I may have spent my whole life learning to be ignorant."

"Or," Ji Gong suggested gently, "you've spent many years gathering ingredients. Perhaps it's time to learn how to cook."

The metaphor hit Wen with startling clarity. He had indeed gathered ingredients: vast stores of knowledge, analytical skills, understanding of human nature and social systems. But he had never learned to combine them into something that could nourish anyone else.

"You speak as if wisdom were... food," Wen said, testing this new way of thinking. "Something meant to be shared rather than hoarded."

"Isn't it?" Ji Gong replied. "What good is a recipe that no one cooks? What value is knowledge that never feeds hungry minds or solves real problems?"

The conversation continued around them, but Wen found himself only half-listening, his mind reeling with implications. If Ji Gong was right, then everything Wen had built his life around (the careful preservation of classical learning, the rigorous analysis of theoretical problems, the elegant debates that impressed colleagues but helped no one) was not just useless but actively harmful. It was wisdom turned into a luxury item, available only to those wealthy enough to afford years of study and disconnected from the lives it was supposedly meant to improve.

That night, Wen sat in his chambers surrounded by the texts that had shaped his life. Thousands of pages of commentary, analysis, and theoretical wisdom surrounded him like beautiful cages, containing truths that had never been allowed to breathe free air or touch human need. The room smelled of aged paper and expensive sandalwood incense, its silence broken only by the distant sound of night watchmen calling the hours.

He thought of the little girl's simple question, of the former bandits' practical wisdom, of the monk who somehow made philosophy as natural as breathing. Most disturbing of all, he thought about his students: those bright young men preparing to govern an empire they had never truly seen.

Sleep refused to come. Instead, Wen found himself walking the corridors of his memory, revisiting years of scholarly achievement that suddenly seemed hollow. How many papers had he written that no one outside academia had read? How many insights had he developed that helped no one beyond his fellow scholars? How many students had he trained to perpetuate the same disconnection from reality that had trapped him?

But beneath the despair, something else was stirring: a spark of possibility that grew brighter as the night wore on. If Ji Gong was right about ingredients and cooking, then perhaps his lifetime of study wasn't entirely wasted. Perhaps all that accumulated knowledge could be transformed into something useful, something that could actually serve the people it was meant to benefit.

By dawn, he had made a decision that would scandalize the academy and transform his understanding of what it meant to be truly learned.

When his advanced class assembled for their usual morning lecture on administrative theory, they found their teacher waiting not in the familiar classroom but at the academy's front gates. Wen stood in the morning sunlight, his scholar's robes immaculate but his expression unlike anything his students had seen before: determined, almost excited, with an energy that crackled in the air around him.

"Today," Scholar Wen announced as his bewildered students gathered around him, "we're going to conduct an experiment. We're going to discover whether our years of study have produced any wisdom that can actually help people."

Wei Sin, quick to articulate what others were thinking, raised his hand uncertainly. "Master, what about our preparation for the examinations? We're supposed to review the Seven Classic Essays on Administrative Harmony."

"The essays will wait," Wen replied, speaking with conviction that surprised even him. "But the people we're supposedly preparing to serve won't. Today, each of you will spend time with a different family in the city, helping with their work, understanding their challenges, and then returning to discuss what governance might actually mean to people who live it rather than theorize about it."

The reaction from his students was immediate and varied. Some looked excited by the prospect of leaving their books for real-world experience. Others appeared horrified at the suggestion that their elevated education should involve manual labor or association with common people.

"But Master," protested Wei Sin, his face pale with shock, "surely this is beneath our station? We're training to be administrators, not laborers."

Wei Sin's voice carried particular belligerence, his family's recent elevation to minor nobility making him especially protective of his scholarly status. His father had climbed from merchant origins through examination success, and Wei Sin felt the weight of maintaining that hard-won respectability.

The question that had been forming in Wen's mind crystallized into perfect clarity. "Are we?" he asked. "Because if our training doesn't help us understand the people we're meant to serve, then we're training to be parasites, not administrators."

The word hit the group like a physical blow. Zhang Ming's face went blank with shock, while several other students looked around seeking escape from this sudden philosophical crisis.

"Master Wen," Ren Zixuan said quietly, "what you're suggesting... it challenges everything we've been taught about proper scholarly conduct."

"Yes," Wen agreed, feeling a strange lightness as he abandoned the weight of a lifetime's assumptions. "It does. And perhaps that's exactly what our scholarly conduct needs: a challenge that forces it to prove its worth in the real world."

The walk through Hangzhou's streets that followed was unlike anything in the academy's distinguished history. Twenty young scholars, trained to debate abstract principles in marble halls, found themselves scattered throughout the city's working districts: helping in rice shops, observing tax collection procedures, assisting with dock work, learning how legal disputes were actually resolved outside courtrooms.

Wen spent his day with Master Bo's weaving family, while Wei Sin accompanied him to the same household. The young scholar had arrived with barely concealed disdain. His fine robes and careful posture marked his resistance to this 'demeaning' task. But his attitude was about to change dramatically.

The workshop assaulted his senses immediately: the sharp tang of mulberry bark dye mixing with the earthy scent of raw silk, the sweet fragrance of sandalwood oil used to condition the threads, and underneath it all, the honest smell of wood shavings and human labor. The rhythmic clacking of the loom provided a steady percussion that seemed to mock the refined silence of marble halls. Above the main loom hung red paper cutouts for good fortune, and a small shrine to the Silk Goddess held offerings of rice wine and fresh chrysanthemums.

"The forms ask for information that doesn't exist," Master Bo explained patiently as Wen struggled to understand how his elegant administrative theories translated into daily frustration for actual people. "They want precise projections of future production, but how can I predict what orders I'll receive?

They require documentation of training methods that have been passed down father to son for generations. How do you write down something that lives in your hands and heart?"

As the day progressed, Wen found himself seeing his own academic work through entirely new eyes. The administrative frameworks he had spent years perfecting were beautiful in theory but nightmarish in practice, creating barriers rather than solutions, generating bureaucracy rather than efficiency.

"Master Bo," Wen said thoughtfully, "would it be possible for my student to spend some time learning your craft? I think he would benefit from understanding how skilled work actually functions."

Master Bo nodded graciously. "Of course, honored scholar. Li Hua can show him the basics of threading." He called to his daughter at the main loom.

Wei Sin approached reluctantly, clearly uncomfortable with this hands-on assignment. But when Li Hua looked up from her loom where delicate silk threads were taking shape under her skilled fingers, Wei Sin's scholarly composure vanished entirely. Her dark eyes assessed the newcomer with calm intelligence while he struggled to remember how to speak.

Li Hua had noticed the young scholar's presence with amusement rather than awe. She had seen enough merchants' sons and minor officials to recognize the type: educated, privileged, and utterly convinced of their own superiority. His careful posture and pristine robes marked him as someone who had never doubted his place in the world's hierarchy.

But when he stumbled over a Du Fu quote, a poem she had memorized while learning to read by candlelight after long days at the loom, she felt a spark of mischief. Perhaps this proud young man needed to learn that wisdom wasn't the exclusive property of marble halls. Her gentle correction was both a test and an invitation: would he retreat into wounded pride, or find the humility to learn?

Wei Sin felt like a man who had been reading poetry his entire life suddenly hearing it sung.

"You read poetry?" Wei Sin asked, his scholarly arrogance momentarily forgotten.

"Why shouldn't I?" she replied with a smile that held gentle challenge. "Because I work with silk instead of scrolls? Beauty exists in many forms, Master Scholar. Perhaps more than you've been taught to see."

As Li Hua began teaching him the threading work, Wei Sin's soft scholar's hands, accustomed only to silk and jade, fumbled with the rough hemp threads. The coarse fibers scratched against his palms, and the constant tension required to maintain proper thread alignment made his fingers ache in ways years of calligraphy practice had never prepared him for.

For the first time in his privileged life, Wei Sin found himself wanting desperately to impress someone who seemed entirely unimpressed by his credentials.

Their afternoon was interrupted by the arrival of Scholar Gao, who appeared at the workshop entrance looking deeply uncomfortable. "Wen," he said urgently, "you need to return to the academy immediately. Dean Ma has summoned you to his office."

As Wen reluctantly departed with Scholar Gao, Wei Sin made the decision to remain at the workshop...

That evening, as the sun set over Hangzhou, Wen found his students scattered throughout the Drunken Phoenix, engaged in animated conversations with the families they had been assigned to help. Wei Sin sat with Master Bo but kept glancing toward the door, hoping Li Hua might appear. The day's work had stained his scholar's robes, but for the first time, he didn't mind.

Zhang Ming was deep in conversation with a street vendor, taking notes not for academic purposes but to understand the economic pressures that shaped daily life in the city.

Most remarkable of all was Ren Zixuan, the quiet student who rarely spoke in class, now holding a sick child while its mother prepared medicine, his formal reserve completely dissolved in the face of immediate human need.

"Master!" Wei Sin called out when he spotted his teacher. "You must hear what Master Bo has been telling me about the tax collection system. The theoretical models we studied bear no resemblance to how it actually works!"

As his students enthusiastically shared discoveries that had transformed their understanding of governance in a single day, Wen felt something settle into place in his chest: a sense of rightness that had nothing to do with academic approval and everything to do with education that actually educated.

"Your students seem to be learning quickly," came a familiar voice. Ji Gong had appeared as if materialized from the evening air, carrying two cups of wine.

"They're learning what I should have been teaching them all along," Wen replied, accepting the offered cup. "The difference between knowing about the world and understanding it."

"I take it word of your experiment reached the academy administrators?" Ji Gong asked, pouring more wine for his friend.

Wen accepted the cup gratefully. "Dean Ma summoned me. The reaction was swift and predictably outraged." He took a long sip before continuing. "An elderly scholar whose family has held positions in the imperial bureaucracy for seven generations does not take kindly to having his methods questioned."

"And what did he say?"

Wen settled back, recounting the confrontation that had sealed his fate at the academy. "I was barely through his office door before he began his lecture," he said with a wry smile.

"Scholar Wen," Dean Ma said, his voice tight with disapproval as he paced behind his rosewood desk, "I've received reports of your... unconventional... teaching methods. Sending students to work alongside common laborers? Abandoning classical texts for manual labor? This is not the Imperial Academy way."

Wen stood in the dean's office, surrounded by the symbols of academic authority (rare books, calligraphy scrolls, jade ornaments that spoke of imperial favor) and felt nothing but weariness for the world they represented.

"Perhaps," Wen replied calmly, "the Imperial Academy way needs examination. When did we decide that education meant separation from the world rather than engagement with it?"

Dean Ma's face flushed with indignation. "When we realized that proper governance requires elevation above common concerns, not immersion in them! How can our graduates maintain appropriate authority if they've been reduced to the level of those they're meant to govern?"

It was a fundamental question that struck at the heart of everything Wen had been reconsidering. The empire's administrative system was built on the assumption that wisdom flowed downward from educated elites to ignorant masses, that authority came from distance and difference rather than understanding and service.

"Dean Ma," Wen said, choosing his words carefully, "with

respect, what if authority based on separation from people produces worse results than authority based on understanding them?"

The argument that followed would be remembered in academy circles for years to come. Dean Ma cited centuries of tradition, the proven success of imperial administrative methods, the dangers of contaminating scholarly purity with common concerns. Wen found himself defending ideas he had only begun to understand, but defending them with a passion that surprised both men.

"You're talking about destroying everything this academy stands for," Dean Ma said finally, his voice heavy with the weight of institutional authority.

"I'm talking about fulfilling everything this academy claims to stand for," Wen replied. "When did learning to serve the people become about avoiding the people? When did wisdom become something too precious to share with those who need it most?"

The conversation ended with an ultimatum: return to conventional teaching methods or seek employment elsewhere. The dean's words were delivered with the cold finality of absolute institutional power, but they felt strangely liberating to Wen's ears.

"And what will you do now?" Ji Gong asked. "It sounds like the dean made his position quite clear."

Wen thought deeply, looking around the tavern, taking in the sight of his students discovering that real learning happened when they stopped protecting themselves from the world and started engaging with it completely. For the first time in his career, he had felt like a teacher whose work actually mattered.

"I think," he said slowly, tasting the possibility as he spoke it, "I'm going to start a different kind of school. One where philosophy meets practice, where wisdom serves people rather than preserving itself, where students learn to be useful rather than merely educated."

"A dangerous proposition," Ji Gong said with a smile that held both warning and encouragement. "The kind that could change everything."

"Yes," Wen agreed, and for the first time in three decades, he felt like a scholar whose learning might actually matter to someone beyond himself. "Exactly that kind."

As Scholar Wen was drawn back into discussions with other students, Wei Sin found himself seeking out Ji Gong at a quieter corner of the tavern, his usual scholarly confidence replaced by obvious uncertainty.

"Master Ji," Wei Sin began hesitantly, then stopped, clearly struggling with how to voice what was troubling him. "Today at Master Bo's workshop, something unexpected happened. I found myself... affected by more than just the lessons about governance." He paused, then continued more quietly. "His daughter, Li Hua. She corrected my recitation of Du Fu, gently, but she knew the poem better than I did. And when she spoke about her silk designs, about the patterns she creates... I found myself thinking that perhaps there are forms of artistry I've never considered." He paused, clearly struggling with unfamiliar emotions. "How does a scholar approach someone whose wisdom comes from silk looms rather than scrolls? What if she finds my education more barrier than bridge?"

"Boy," Widow Tan interrupted from a nearby table, setting down her cup with a decisive clink, "you think too much and feel too little. You want to court a girl? Stop worrying about what makes you different and start paying attention to what makes her special. Ask about her work like it matters. Listen to her thoughts like they're worth hearing. Treat her family with respect instead of looking down your nose at them."

Wei Sin sat in stunned silence, his carefully ordered world of rules and precedents suddenly seeming irrelevant in the face of such straightforward wisdom. "But surely there are proper protocols, established methods…"

"Protocols?" Widow Tan laughed. "Child, love isn't a classical text you can memorize. It's like vegetables in the market. You examine them carefully, and if they're good, you don't haggle over whether they came from the right kind of soil."

Ji Gong grinned at Wei Sin's obvious disorientation. "The widow speaks from deeper learning than any courtship manual, young brother. Perhaps the question isn't how a scholar should approach a weaver's daughter, but how one human being shows respect and genuine interest to another."

"Master Ji," Wei Sin added hesitantly, "there's another concern. My family… they have expectations about who I should marry. Someone from a scholarly family, someone who would advance our social position."

"Ah," Ji Gong nodded. "And what do you think is more important advancing your family's position in society, or advancing your own growth as a human being?"

Wei Sin was quiet for a moment. "I… I never thought to ask that question before."

"The best questions," Ji Gong said gently, "are often the ones we've never thought to ask."

The next day Wei Sin faced his own transformation. When he appeared at the workshop door with his scholar's robes exchanged for simple work clothes, Li Hua felt a flutter of surprise. She had expected him to disappear back to his marble halls, wounded pride keeping him safely distant from their humble silk workshop.

Instead, here he stood, asking her father how he might best help with the day's work. When Master Bo assigned him to assist with the more delicate threading, work that required patience rather than strength, Wei Sin accepted without protest.

As Li Hua watched him struggle with tasks that her hands had mastered years ago, she noticed something that impressed her more than any scholarly achievement: he was genuinely trying to learn, not simply enduring an obligation. When he asked her quiet advice about the tension of the threads, she found herself answering with less teasing and more teaching.

Perhaps, she thought as she watched his careful concentration, there was more to this scholar than silk robes and borrowed verses.

In the weeks that followed, word spread throughout Hangzhou of a new kind of education being offered in the rooms above the tea shop. Students came not to memorize ancient texts but to learn how those texts could illuminate modern problems. They studied not in isolation but in service, discovering that wisdom was something you gave away rather than hoarded.

The Imperial Academy officially censured Scholar Wen and struck his name from their rolls. But his students, as they spread throughout the province in administrative positions, became known for an unusual combination of scholarly depth and practical effectiveness.

Through the changing season, Wei Sin became Master Bo's most dedicated student-assistant, learning not just the silk trade but discovering that wisdom lived as fully in skilled hands as in scholarly texts. His courtship of Li Hua proceeded with the careful patience of a man who had learned that the greatest treasures were earned through service, not claimed through status.

When Wei Sin finally told his parents about Li Hua, the reaction was exactly what he had feared. His father, who had climbed from merchant origins to minor official status through examination success, saw his son's choice as a step backward.

"A weaver's daughter?" his father said, his voice tight with disappointment. "Son, we've worked too hard to elevate this family's position for you to marry beneath your station."

But Wei Sin had changed too much to be swayed by old fears. "Father, I'm not marrying beneath my station. I'm marrying someone whose wisdom and character elevate mine. Master Bo's family is prosperous and respected. Li Hua reads poetry, creates intricate designs, and understands both beauty and commerce. What more could you want in a daughter-in-law?"

His mother, who had been quietly observing, finally spoke. "Show us," she said simply. "Bring her to meet us. Let us see this remarkable woman who has so changed our scholarly son."

Li Hua's grace and intelligence won over Wei Sin's family from their first meeting. And when she accepted his marriage proposal, it was not for his scholarly achievements, but for the genuine man he had become. Their union, which his parents blessed with genuine respect, taught them all the true meaning of a worthy partnership.

And in taverns throughout the empire, the story spread of the scholar who learned from a monk that the highest education was not in knowing more than others, but in serving them better than you ever thought possible.

The revolution in learning had begun with a simple question

from a little girl about her grandmother's pain. Sometimes, Scholar Wen would reflect in later years, the most profound transformations started with the most basic human needs.

Chapter 12

The Final Teaching

Rumors traveled through the district like ripples on still water, each circle growing wider and more urgent as word spread that Ji Gong was going to be summoned to appear before the Provincial Governor himself.

Within the hour, the news had reached Master Bo's silk workshop, where Wei Sin was helping Li Hua adjust the tension on a new loom. She stopped her work immediately, her hands frozen on the delicate threads.

"This is about more than one monk," she said. "If they can silence him, what happens to everything he's built? What happens to people like us who've learned to see beyond the old boundaries?"

Wei Sin's face hardened with a resolve his former classmates would hardly have recognized. "Then we don't let them silence him. Scholar Wen always taught us that ideas belong to everyone once they're spoken. They can summon Ji Gong, but they can't summon the truth he's shown us."

Iron Wolf wiped sweat from his brow as he finished hammering the last bent wheel rim back into shape, another repair job that had brought him from the blacksmith shop to the bustling docks, then turned to face his fellow workers with grim understanding. "Brothers," he said to the mixed group of former bandits and lifelong laborers who had become his closest companions, "do you remember what we were before he found us?"

Stone nodded slowly. "Thieves hiding in caves, taking what we needed and calling it survival."

"And now?"

"Now we build things," said Young Crane, gesturing toward the dozen projects they'd completed that week alone. "We protect what we once would have stolen. We've become the men we always could have been."

"Exactly," Iron Wolf said. "Which means we owe him a debt that can't be measured in silver. If they want to judge him, they'll have to judge us too."

By midday, an impromptu gathering had formed in the tavern's main room. Ji Gong had left earlier to help some refugees find shelter, and word of the rumors had drawn concerned citizens to discuss what might happen next. Scholar Wen arrived with several of his students, their faces showing a mixture of concern and determination that would have been impossible in their marble halls just months before.

"Master," said Zhang Ming, the serious young man who had once worried only about examination scores, "what can we do? We're not officials or nobles. We have no influence with governors."

"Don't we?" Wen replied, looking around at the assembled

crowd. "Look at this room. Former criminals, current merchants, scholars and laborers, refugees and citizens, all sitting together, planning together, caring about the same things. If that's not influence, what is?"

Master Zhao stepped forward, still holding his son's hand though the boy was now seventeen and taller than his father. "Ji Gong saved more than my child," he said, his words reaching clearly across the room. "He saved the man I was becoming: bitter, suspicious, caring only for my own family's welfare. He showed me that the boundaries I thought protected us were actually imprisoning us."

"So what do we do?" asked Widow Tan, who had closed her vegetable stall early to join the gathering. "March to the temple? Demand they release him?"

"No!" said a voice from the back of the room. Master Hui had entered unnoticed, his Buddhist robes marking him as distinctly out of place in the secular gathering. Word of the community's concern had reached the temple, and the old monk had come to offer what guidance he could. "That would only prove their point about disorder and disruption."

He moved through the crowd until he stood where everyone could see him. "But there is something we can do. We can be living proof that his way works. When he faces judgment, we can show them what he's actually created."

"How?" Wei Sin asked.

"By continuing to be who he helped us become. By proving that compassion creates order, not chaos. By demonstrating that when people are trusted, they become trustworthy. By showing that his influence wasn't temporary disruption but permanent transformation."

The room fell silent as the implications settled over them.

They weren't just spectators to Ji Gong's trial, they were evidence in his defense.

"Then let's give them evidence they can't ignore," Iron Wolf said grimly. "Let's show them what a district looks like when it's built on hope instead of fear."

The summons came the next morning when the autumn air carried the first hint of winter's approach. Brother Wuxin arrived at the Drunken Phoenix with an official scroll bearing the seal of Lingyin Temple, his face grave with the weight of unwelcome duty.

"Ji Gong," he said formally, using the name by which the monk was now known throughout Hangzhou, "Abbot Yuan Kong requests your immediate presence at the temple. The matter is… urgent."

Ji Gong looked up from his breakfast. It was a simple bowl of rice shared with a family of refugees who had arrived in the city nights before. His face showed no surprise, as if he had been expecting this moment for some time.

"Urgent for whom?" he asked mildly. "For the abbot, or for the refugees who need shelter before the winter rains begin?"

"For you," Wuxin replied, his voice tight with barely controlled frustration. "The Provincial Governor himself has heard reports of your… activities. There are questions about your conduct that only the abbot can address."

The refugees, a young couple with two small children driven from their village by flood and failed harvests, looked up with alarm. In the few days since Ji Gong had found them sleeping in a doorway, he had not only provided them with food and temporary shelter but had begun organizing the community to help them establish a new life in the city.

"Master Ji," the young father said quietly, "if you're in trouble because of us…"

"Old friend," Ji Gong replied, placing a reassuring hand on the man's shoulder, "I'm not in trouble because of you. I'm in trouble because there are people who believe helping you is wrong. There's a significant difference."

He rose from the table, brushing rice grains from his patched robes with the unhurried movements of someone at peace with whatever might come. "Brother Wuxin, shall we go see what the Provincial Governor finds so disturbing about refugees having enough to eat?"

The walk to Lingyin Temple became an unintended procession through the heart of the transformation Ji Gong had helped create. As they moved through the streets, the evidence of change was impossible to ignore, even for someone as determined to remain disapproving as Brother Wuxin.

At the first intersection, they encountered Mu the carpenter organizing a group of workers to repair storm damage to Widow Tan's roof. What caught Wuxin's attention wasn't the work itself, but the composition of the crew: two former bandits, a scholar, a silk merchant, and three dock workers, all laboring together without regard for their vastly different social positions.

"Master Ji!" called out Stone, wiping sweat from his brow as he secured a beam. "Heard about your appointment with the governor. Don't worry about us here, we'll keep things running smooth while you're gone."

"Just as you have been," Ji Gong replied with genuine warmth. "The work continues whether I'm here or not. That's how it should be."

Wuxin watched this exchange with growing confusion. "These men speak to you as equals," he observed as they continued walking. "Where is the proper deference a monk should receive?"

"Brother," Ji Gong replied, "what is more respectful? Empty ceremony, or trust that the work we started together will continue without me?"

Three streets over, they passed the small school that Scholar Wen had established above a tea shop. Through the open windows came the sound of discussion rather than rote recitation. A young voice was asking, "But how does this help the farmers we visited yesterday?" while an older voice patiently explained the practical applications of classical administrative theory.

"Learning that serves people instead of preserving itself," Ji Gong noted, seeing Wuxin's startled expression. "Revolutionary, isn't it?"

At the market square, they were approached by a group of children from mixed social backgrounds, their clothes marking them as everything from merchants' sons to laborers' daughters. They surrounded Ji Gong with the easy familiarity of those who had never been taught to fear difference.

"Master Ji," said a young girl, "is it true you have to go talk to the big officials about helping people?"

"It's true, Little Flower. They have questions about whether helping people is the right thing for a monk to do."

The children exchanged glances with the solemn wisdom that sometimes emerges from young minds. "That's a silly question," announced a boy whose silk robes marked him as from a wealthy family. "Of course helping people is right. My father says you helped him remember that having money means nothing if your neighbors are sad."

"Sometimes the clearest wisdom comes from the simplest hearts," Ji Gong remarked, but loud enough for Wuxin to hear.

As they approached the temple district, they passed the workshop where Wei Sin and Li Hua were working side by side, their marriage having become a symbol of how social barriers could dissolve without destroying social fabric. Wei Sin looked up from the loom where he was learning silk production from his wife's expert hands.

"Ji Gong," he called through the window, "whatever they ask you today, remember that some of us became better people because you showed us it was possible."

"And some of us," Li Hua added with a smile, "found love because you taught us to see beyond appearances."

Wuxin's step faltered slightly. "That young man," he said, noting Wei Sin's fine features and educated speech, "he speaks like a scholar, yet he works with his hands. And the way he looks at that woman, with such respect for her knowledge..."

"A scholar discovering that wisdom exists in many forms," Ji Gong replied. "Amazing what happens when we stop assuming education makes us superior to those who work with their hands."

They were now within sight of the temple gates, but their progress was slowed by a final encounter that would stay with Wuxin long after the day's events concluded. An elderly beggar, his clothes clean but patched, approached them with the careful dignity of someone who had learned to respect himself.

"Master," the old man said with a deep bow, "I heard about your summons. I wanted you to know that because of you, I haven't begged for food in six months. The work you helped me find, the community that accepted me, the chance to contribute instead of just surviving, these things gave me back my humanity."

He straightened, looking directly at Wuxin. "Honored

brother, I don't know what charges they've brought against this man, but I can tell you what he's guilty of: making me remember that I'm a human being worthy of respect and capable of useful work."

As the old man walked away with the steady gait of someone who had purpose in his life, Wuxin turned to Ji Gong with an expression that mixed confusion and something approaching understanding.

"I came here expecting to escort a disgraced monk to face justice," he said slowly. "Instead, I find myself walking through what appears to be a community transformed. How do I reconcile these two realities?"

"Perhaps," Ji Gong suggested as they reached the temple gates, "the question isn't how to reconcile them, but how to choose between them. Does the appearance of disgrace matter more than the reality of transformation?"

Brother Wuxin had no answer. The doubt growing in his eyes suggested that Ji Gong had already won his most important convert - not through arguments, but through the living evidence of what compassion could accomplish.

Before Wuxin could respond, the temple doors opened and Master Hui appeared, his aged face lined with worry and something that might have been regret.

"Daoji," he said, using the monk's original name, "you've come."

"Of course I've come, old teacher. When the Provincial Governor wishes to discuss philosophy, how could I refuse such an honor?"

They were escorted through the familiar courtyards to the abbot's garden, where a scene awaited them that made clear the gravity of the situation. Abbot Yuan Kong knelt in formal posture before a silk pavilion that had been erected for the occasion. Within the pavilion sat a figure in robes of imperial yellow. This was Governor Shen Shimin himself, a man whose word could elevate temples to prosperity or reduce them to forgotten ruins.

Beside the governor stood Magistrate Wang Jinshan, his face showing barely concealed satisfaction at finally having the troublesome monk brought before higher authority. Several other officials completed the assembly, their expressions ranging from curiosity to stern disapproval.

"So," Governor Shen said without preamble as Ji Gong approached and offered the minimum bow required by protocol, "you are the monk who has been turning Hangzhou upside down with wine and charity."

"I am Ji Gong," he replied simply. "I am a monk who has discovered that wine and charity have remarkable power to turn things right-side up."

Shocked whispers spread among the officials at this audacious response to imperial authority. Governor Shen's eyebrows rose slightly, but his expression remained unreadable.

"Magistrate Wang has filed reports describing your activities," the governor continued. "Drinking alcohol in public. Consorting with criminals. Disrupting established social hierarchies. Encouraging servants to forget their proper deference to their masters."

"All true," Ji Gong acknowledged cheerfully. "Though I would describe the last item as encouraging people to remember that we're all human beings deserving of basic dignity."

"And you see no problem with such activities? No conflict with your monastic vows?"

157

Ji Gong was quiet for a moment, looking around the garden where he had once faced judgment for feeding the hungry. The carefully arranged stones and pruned trees seemed different now, still beautiful, but somehow smaller than he remembered.

"Your Excellency," he said finally, "you accuse me of abandoning Buddhist teaching, yet everything I do follows the Buddha's Noble Eightfold Path. Perhaps the question is not whether I'm a proper Buddhist, but whether Buddhism should serve temples or serve humanity."

The officials exchanged glances and hushed words. Governor Shen leaned forward, his interest clearly engaged. "Explain this Eightfold Path defense of yours, monk. Let us hear how drinking wine and consorting with criminals serves the Buddha's teaching."

Ji Gong stepped closer to the pavilion. His words rang clearly in the garden's perfect acoustics. "The first path is Right Understanding. I understand that all beings suffer, and that my purpose is to relieve that suffering wherever I find it, not to preserve my own comfort while others despair."

"The second is Right Intention. My intention has always been compassion, not disruption. I seek to end suffering, not create chaos. If my methods disturb those who profit from others' pain, perhaps the problem lies not with my intentions but with their resistance to change."

Magistrate Wang shifted uncomfortably. "Pretty words, but your actions…"

"The third path," Ji Gong continued, his voice growing stronger, "is Right Speech. I speak truth to power and comfort to the afflicted. I use words to heal, not harm. When I tell a tax collector to remember his own mother's struggles, am I not practicing Right Speech? When I encourage a reformed bandit that he can become better than his past, am I not speaking rightly?"

Governor Shen held up a hand to silence Wang's objection. "Continue, monk. You have our attention."

"The fourth path is Right Action. Every action I take serves those in need. Feeding the hungry, sheltering the homeless, reforming criminals, teaching compassion to those who have forgotten it. Tell me, Your Excellency, which of these actions violates Buddhist teaching?"

The garden fell silent except for the gentle splash of the ornamental stream. Several officials exchanged glances, clearly recognizing the strength of his theological argument.

"The fifth path is Right Livelihood. I live simply, take nothing for myself, and devote my life to service. I own no property, accumulate no wealth, seek no position or honor. How is this wrong livelihood? Because I refuse to live it within temple walls while people suffer outside them?"

Abbot Yuan Kong's face showed a mixture of pride and concern. This was theology he could not easily refute, presented by the student who had once been his greatest challenge.

"The sixth path is Right Effort. I make constant effort to cultivate compassion and wisdom, not just for myself but for all beings. Is it not right effort to work tirelessly for the welfare of others? To refuse the ease of withdrawal when engagement serves the greater good?"

"The seventh path is Right Mindfulness. I remain mindful of suffering wherever I encounter it, never turning away from those in need. When I see a beggar, I'm mindful of hunger. When I see a criminal, I'm mindful of desperation. When I see the wealthy hoarding while others starve, I'm mindful of the inequality that breeds both greed and resentment."

Ji Gong paused, looking directly at Governor Shen. "And the eighth path is Right Concentration. But here is where my understanding differs from conventional teaching. My meditation is not escape from the world but deeper engagement with it. I concentrate not on emptiness but on fullness, the full reality of human need and the full possibility of human compassion."

The silence that followed was profound. Governor Shen sat back in his chair, his expression thoughtful and clearly troubled.

"You present us with a sophisticated argument," he said finally. "But tell me this: if every monk followed your interpretation, what would become of monastic order? What would become of the temples, the preserved teachings, the centuries of accumulated wisdom?"

"Your Excellency," Ji Gong replied, "I would ask you this in return: what good is preserved wisdom if it's never applied? What value are temples if they become museums of unused compassion? What purpose does accumulated teaching serve if it creates scholars of suffering rather than healers of it?"

His words encompassed the world beyond these walls, where the district he had helped transform thrived. "The Buddha left his palace not to build a more beautiful palace, but to discover truth in the world of actual experience. He didn't teach the Eightfold Path so monks could perfect themselves in isolation, but so they could perfect themselves through service."

"Most importantly," Ji Gong continued, with the conviction that only experience brings, "the Buddha's final words were 'work out your salvation with diligence.' Not 'preserve your purity with withdrawal,' not 'maintain your comfort with separation,' but work, with diligence, in the world where salvation is needed most."

Governor Shen was quiet for several minutes, his gaze moving between the assembled officials, the peaceful temple buildings, and the monk whose theological argument had just called into question not only monastic practice but the entire relationship between spiritual authority and social responsibility.

"Ji Gong," he said finally, "your defense is... compelling. You have used the Buddha's own teaching to justify methods that appear to contradict Buddhist tradition. Yet your results speak for themselves. Your district prospers while others struggle with crime, poverty, and social discord."

"Your Excellency," Magistrate Wang interjected, his voice tight with desperation, "consider the precedent this sets. If word spreads that the empire tolerates monks who defy authority, what happens when every temple decides to ignore imperial edicts? What happens when every district starts 'reforming' criminals instead of punishing them according to law?"

"Magistrate Wang," Ji Gong replied calmly, "you speak as if compassion were contagious. I certainly hope it is. But tell me, what terrifies you more: the possibility that other districts might become as prosperous and peaceful as this one, or the possibility that your methods of control might no longer be necessary?"

Wang's face flushed. "You speak of success in one small district, but what of the empire? If servants everywhere begin demanding equal treatment, if established hierarchies collapse, if every beggar expects charity as a right, how does the government maintain order across ten thousand li?"

"Perhaps," Ji Gong said clearly, "the question isn't how to

maintain the old order, but whether the old order is worth maintaining. You fear what happens if people are treated with dignity. I fear what happens if they continue to be treated without it."

"You've given beggars the same respect as nobles, haven't you?" Wang said with contempt.

"Yes," Ji Gong said simply. "I've treated people like people. I can see how that might be confusing to someone who's spent his career treating them like categories."

Governor Shen raised a hand to silence the growing argument. "Monk," he said, his voice carrying the absolute authority of imperial appointment, "your methods may have produced temporary benefits, but they threaten the fundamental order on which civilization depends. Social hierarchies exist for good reason. If everyone believes they deserve equal treatment, if all distinctions of rank and merit are erased, what prevents society from collapsing into chaos?"

The question hung in the air like the temple's evening incense, heavy with centuries of accumulated assumption about how the world must work. Ji Gong felt the scrutiny of every watching face. Not just those of the officials who would determine his fate, but those of his former brothers, his old teacher, and the representatives of an order he had once sought to serve.

"Your Excellency," he said, his voice quiet but carrying clearly in the garden's perfect acoustics, "may I ask you a question in return?"

The governor nodded.

"In your travels throughout the province, in your experience governing different districts, have you found that people work harder when they're afraid or when they're hopeful? Do they serve more faithfully when they're forced or when they're valued? Are they more honest when they're punished for dishonesty or when they're rewarded for truth?"

Governor Shen was silent for a long moment, his expression thoughtful. "You suggest that hierarchy based on fear is less effective than... what? Community based on mutual respect?"

"I suggest that the order you're trying to preserve is actually disorder disguised as stability. When one person's dignity depends on another's humiliation, when one family's prosperity requires another's poverty, when one class's security demands another's fear, that's not order. That's barely controlled chaos."

Ji Gong looked beyond the temple walls, beyond which lay the thriving district he had helped transform. "Real order comes when everyone has a stake in everyone else's wellbeing. Real stability emerges when people work together instead of against each other. Real civilization begins when we stop trying to control human nature and start trusting it."

The silence that followed was broken by an unexpected voice. Abbot Yuan Kong, who had remained silent throughout the confrontation, rose from his formal position and stepped forward.

"Your Excellency," he said, his aged voice carrying the weight of forty years in religious service, "I have governed this temple for nearly three decades. I have seen many monks come and go, many interpretations of Buddhist teaching, many attempts to serve the Buddha's purpose in the world."

He paused, looking at Ji Gong with an expression that mixed sorrow and pride in equal measure. "Brother Daoji, also known as Ji Gong, was the most troublesome novice I ever encountered. He broke rules, challenged authority, and disrupted our carefully maintained order. I exiled him to the mountains, hoping solitude would teach him proper discipline."

Another pause, longer this time. "Instead, it taught him something I had never learned in all my years of study and meditation. It taught him that the Buddha's compassion is not something to be preserved in temples but something to be lived in the world. That wisdom is not something to be hoarded by the wise but something to be shared with whoever needs it most."

Governor Shen leaned forward, his interest clearly engaged. "And what is your assessment of his... methods?"

Before the abbot could respond, Brother Wuxin stepped forward, his voice quiet but carrying clearly across the garden. "Your Excellency, I came this morning to escort what I believed was a disgraced monk to face justice. But in walking through the district he serves, I witnessed something I had not expected: order created through compassion, not control. Community built on trust, not fear. If this is disruption, then perhaps we need to reconsider what we mean by proper order."

Master Hui stepped forward with the measured dignity of a lifelong teacher. "Your Excellency, I have instructed this monk in the Buddha's teaching since he first entered our gates as a troubled young man. I taught him the Four Noble Truths, watched him struggle with their meaning, and thought I had failed when he could not find peace within our walls." He paused, his aged voice growing stronger. "Today I understand that I did not fail as a teacher. I succeeded beyond my hopes. He learned the dharma so completely that he had to live it in the world where it was needed most. The Buddha himself left his palace not to build a more beautiful palace, but to serve all beings. How can we fault a monk for following that example?"

"I believe," Abbot Yuan Kong said carefully, "that he has become the kind of monk the Buddha intended. Not one who withdraws from suffering to preserve his own purity, but one who enters suffering completely to heal it wherever he finds it."

The governor was quiet for several minutes, his gaze moving between the assembled officials, the peaceful temple buildings, and the monk whose simple presence had somehow called into question everything they thought they knew about order and authority."

"Ji Gong," he said finally, "you present us with a dilemma. Your methods work; that much is undeniable. Your district prospers while others struggle with crime, poverty, and social discord. Yet your approach threatens to undermine the very systems that have maintained peace and stability throughout the empire."

He stood, his yellow robes flowing and sighing like evening wind through pine needles. "Therefore, we offer you a choice. Return to orthodox monastic practice, remain within these temple walls, observe traditional rules, content yourself with conventional charity, and you may continue your religious life without interference."

The alternative hung unspoken in the air, as clear as temple bells in morning silence.

"Or?" Ji Gong asked quietly.

"Or continue as you have been, accepting that your approach may inspire others to challenge established order throughout the province. Accept that you will be seen as a dangerous example of what happens when individual conscience conflicts with social stability."

Ji Gong looked around the garden one last time, and the

magnitude of what he was about to lose settled over him like the evening mist that gathered in these mountains. This place had been his sanctuary, the walls that had protected him while he learned to understand both himself and the world beyond. Here were his brothers in faith, his teacher who had guided him through the hardest questions a soul could face, and the rhythm of prayer and meditation that had shaped every day since his youth.

To leave meant abandoning not just comfort and safety, but belonging itself. No other temple would welcome a monk cast out for defying imperial authority. He would become truly homeless, dependent on the kindness of people who might turn away when supporting him became dangerous. The community he had built could be scattered by official pressure, the students dispersed, the reformed criminals sent back to their mountains, the careful web of trust and cooperation destroyed by those who saw it as a threat to proper order.

But as he looked at the faces surrounding him, Ji Gong saw something that made his choice clear. In Magistrate Wang's eyes, he saw the fear of a man who preferred the misery he could control to the joy he couldn't predict. In Governor Shen's expression, he saw the burden of someone trapped between his conscience and his duty, knowing what was right but constrained by what was expected. Even in some of the other officials, he glimpsed the hunger of people who had forgotten that service could be more satisfying than authority.

These were not evil men, but they were caught in a system that made goodness dangerous and compassion a luxury they couldn't afford. To accept their offer would be to join them in that trap, to become complicit in the very structures that kept people suffering while their potential saviors worried about protocol.

"Your Excellency," he spoke with absolute certainty, "a young man stood in his father's garden, surrounded by wealth and comfort and security, and chose to give it all away in search of something more true. He thought he was sacrificing everything for nothing. But what he discovered was that what looked like nothing was actually everything."

He turned toward Master Hui, whose aged eyes held tears that spoke of pride and loss in equal measure. "Honored teacher, you gave me the tools to understand the Buddha's compassion. Now I must use them as the Buddha intended, in the world where compassion is needed most."

Then he faced Abbot Yuan Kong, the man who had been both leader and adversary, guide and obstacle in his spiritual journey. "Venerable Abbot, I know this choice disappoints you. But I also know you understand it. You've seen what happens when we preserve the teaching instead of living it. Today, I choose to live it, whatever the cost."

Finally, he addressed Governor Shen directly, his voice gentle but unshakeable. "Your Excellency, you offer me the choice between a comfortable lie and an uncomfortable truth. Between preserving an institution and serving its purpose. Between being a perfect monk by the world's definition and being an imperfect human by the Buddha's example."

He moved toward the temple gates with the steady gait of someone walking toward destiny rather than exile. "That's not really a choice at all. A perfect monk who serves only himself is worth nothing. An imperfect human who serves everyone else is worth everything."

As he paused at the threshold between the temple grounds and the world beyond, Ji Gong felt neither sadness nor regret, but rather the profound lightness that comes from finally understanding one's true calling. Behind him lay a life of secure spiritual practice and respected religious authority. Ahead lay uncertainty, danger, and the endless challenges of trying to heal a world that often preferred its wounds to the pain of healing.

But ahead he could see the faces of people who had learned to hope because of him, the voices of those who had discovered their own capacity for goodness, and the infinite possibility that love might indeed prove stronger than fear, that compassion might overcome control, that the wisdom of the heart could transform even the most rigid systems.

"With respect," he said, turning back for one final observation, "you're asking me to choose between being a monk and being Buddhist. I choose Buddhist."

As he walked away from Lingyin Temple for the last time, Ji Gong felt neither sadness nor regret, but rather the lightness that comes from finally understanding one's true calling. Behind him lay a life of comfortable spiritual practice, ahead lay a path of uncertain but authentic service.

A young temple servant who had witnessed the proceedings from the garden's edge had run through the streets with news that Ji Gong had chosen exile over submission. Word of his decision spread through the district like wildfire. By the time he reached the city streets, small groups had already begun gathering at key intersections, their concerned, determined faces touched with defiance.

The first to reach him were Wei Sin and Li Hua, who had been waiting just beyond the temple district. Wei Sin's usual scholarly reserve was nowhere to be found as he rushed forward.

"Master," Wei Sin said, slightly out of breath from running, "we heard what happened. The whole community knows you've been cast out. What do we do now?"

"What you've always done," Ji Gong replied with a smile that held no trace of self-pity. "Continue to be the people you've discovered you can be. My presence was never what made the transformation possible. Your willingness to change was."

Li Hua stepped forward, her eyes bright with unshed tears but her voice steady. "You don't understand. It's not just about continuing what you started. It's about what happens to people like us if they decide to scatter your influence. My husband was a proud, prejudiced scholar before you showed him there was a better way to live. Without your example..."

"Without my example, you'll create your own," Ji Gong interrupted gently. "The love between you two doesn't depend on my blessing. The respect you've learned to show each other, the way you've discovered that different social classes can work together, the children you'll raise to see beyond the boundaries that once seemed absolute, these things belong to you now."

By this time, Iron Wolf had arrived with several of his fellow former bandits, their faces grim with the kind of loyalty that once would have led them to violence. "Ji Gong," Iron Wolf said, his scarred hands clenched at his sides, "just say the word. We know these mountains better than any governor's soldiers. We can make sure you're safe, make sure they leave you alone to continue your work."

The monk looked at these men who had once solved problems with force and felt a deep pride in how far they had traveled from their former selves. "Old friends," he said, "do you hear what you're suggesting? You're offering to return to the shadows, to become outlaws again, to abandon everything you've built here, all to protect me from the consequences of my own choice."

Stone nodded grimly. "That's exactly what we're suggesting. You gave us new lives. The least we can do is risk them to preserve yours."

"And that," Ji Gong said with a warmth that encompassed all of them, "is precisely why I'm not worried about what happens next. Men who were once willing to kill for silver are now willing to sacrifice for principle. If that's not proof that people can change, what is?"

Scholar Wen approached with a group of his students, their expressions showing the determined thoughtfulness that had become their trademark. "Ji Gong," Wen said formally, "we've been discussing the situation. My school exists because you showed me that learning should serve people rather than preserving itself. If the authorities decide to close us down because of our association with you…"

"Then you'll find another building, another way to teach, another method of proving that education works best when it engages with the world," Ji Gong finished. "Scholar Wen, you've become the teacher you were always meant to be. No governor can take that away from you."

Zhang Ming, the serious young man who had grown from academic concerns to social consciousness, stepped forward. "But Master, what about the precedent? If they can silence you, what's to stop them from silencing anyone who challenges the old ways?"

Ji Gong looked around at the growing crowd that had gathered in the street. Former criminals stood beside current merchants, scholars debated with laborers, refugees shared concerns with established citizens. The social boundaries that had once seemed natural and necessary had dissolved so completely that most people no longer even noticed their absence.

"Zhang Ming," he said, his words ringing clearly in the evening air, "look around you. Do you see people who can be easily silenced? Do you see a community that will quietly return to the old ways of fear and separation just because one monk has been sent away?"

The young man followed his gaze, taking in the determined faces, the crossed social lines, the obvious solidarity that connected people who had once seen each other as strangers or threats. His expression slowly shifted from worry to understanding.

"They can silence you," Zhang Ming said with growing conviction, "but they can't silence all of us. And they certainly can't make us forget what we've learned about treating each other with dignity and respect."

"Exactly," Ji Gong said. "What we've discovered together isn't dependent on my presence. It's become part of who you are, all of you. You've learned that former enemies can become friends, that different social classes can work together, that helping others actually makes everyone more prosperous and secure."

Master Zhao appeared at the edge of the crowd, his son Weiming beside him. Both men looked older than their years, marked by the kind of wisdom that comes from seeing one's deepest assumptions proven wrong and discovering something better in their place.

"Ji Gong," Master Zhao said, speaking with the authority of someone who had learned to measure worth by contribution rather than accumulation, "we want you to know that this community doesn't end with your exile. We've sent messages to merchants in other districts, scholars in other cities, officials who've heard about what we've accomplished here. Your ideas are already spreading beyond Hangzhou."

"And more importantly," Weiming added with the passion of youth combined with the wisdom of experience, "we're raising children who will never think it's natural for people to be divided by fear and prejudice. They'll take these ideas to places we've never imagined."

As the sun continued to set, painting the sky in shades of gold and crimson, more people gathered until the street resembled a festival rather than a farewell. Someone produced wine, others brought food, and gradually the somber mood of crisis transformed into something approaching celebration.

"You know what this is, don't you?" asked Widow Tan. "This is proof that what you've taught us works. Instead of scattering in fear when authority threatens us, we're coming together to support each other. Instead of abandoning the changes we've made, we're committing to making them permanent."

Ji Gong looked around at the impromptu gathering and felt a satisfaction deeper than any he had known in his years of formal religious practice. These people didn't need him anymore, not in the way a teacher is needed by students or a leader by followers. They had internalized the lessons, made the principles their own, become the change they had once thought impossible.

"My friends," he said, his voice somehow reaching everyone despite the growing crowd, "when I was young, I thought wisdom was something you acquired through study and preserved through careful practice. Tonight, I understand that real wisdom is something you give away until it becomes so much a part of the world that it no longer needs you to sustain it."

He raised his cup in a toast meant for the entire gathering. "To all of you, who discovered that the greatest adventures aren't about taking what you want, but giving what you have. To the children you're raising, who will think compassion is normal and cooperation is natural. To the future you're creating, where the questions we've struggled with will seem as obsolete as the fears that once divided us."

As the crowd raised their cups in response, their voices creating a harmony that echoed off the surrounding buildings, Ji Gong realized that this wasn't an ending at all. It was a commencement, the moment when the students graduated from needing their teacher and became teachers themselves.

The gathering slowly quieted as people began to return to their homes, each returning to homes and families that had been transformed by the simple recognition that compassion was not weakness but strength, that trust created more security than fear ever could. Ji Gong watched them go with the deep satisfaction of a teacher whose students had surpassed their instruction, a gardener whose seeds had grown into forests that would flourish long after the original planting was forgotten.

As the last stragglers headed home through streets now lit by paper lanterns and alive with the sounds of families sharing evening meals, Ji Gong found himself alone but not lonely, cast out but not abandoned, finished with one life but ready to begin another. Tomorrow would bring new challenges, new opportunities to prove that love was stronger than fear, that hope was more powerful than control, that the wisdom of the heart could indeed transform the world.

But tonight, there was wine to be shared with whoever

needed companionship, stories to be told to whoever needed hope, and the endless wonder of discovering what miracles became possible when you stopped worrying about what was proper and started caring about what was necessary.

The mad monk was truly free at last, and the real adventures were just beginning.

THE END

Comprehensive Reader's Companion

A guide to understanding the Buddhist philosophy, Chinese culture, and historical context of Ji Gong's world

PART I: BUDDHIST PHILOSOPHY & CONCEPTS

The Four Noble Truths

The foundation of Buddhist teaching, introduced by Master Hui in Chapter 3

- **Dukkha** (The Truth of Suffering)
- Life contains suffering, dissatisfaction, and impermanence
- Not just physical pain, but the deeper ache of unfulfilled desire
- The gap between how things are and how we want them to be
- **Tanha** (The Truth of the Cause of Suffering)
- Suffering arises from attachment, craving, and clinging

- Our endless wanting creates a cycle of dissatisfaction
- Includes attachment to people, possessions, ideas, and even our own identity
- **Nirodha** (The Truth of the End of Suffering)
- Suffering can cease through the release of attachments
- Not about eliminating desire, but transforming our relationship to it
- Finding peace with what is, rather than fighting what isn't
- **Magga** (The Truth of the Path)
- The Noble Eightfold Path shows the way to end suffering
- A practical guide for ethical living and mental cultivation
- Balance between extreme indulgence and extreme asceticism

The Noble Eightfold Path

Buddhist practice for ending suffering, used in Ji Gong's defense in Chapter 12

Wisdom (Prajna)

1. **Right Understanding** - Seeing reality clearly; understanding the Four Noble Truths and the interconnectedness of all life

2. **Right Intention** - Commitment to ethical and mental self-improvement; intention of renunciation, good will, and harmlessness

Ethical Conduct (Sila)

3. **Right Speech** - Speaking truthfully and helpfully; avoiding lies, gossip, harsh words, and idle chatter

4. **Right Action** - Ethical conduct; avoiding harm to living beings, stealing, and sexual misconduct

5. **Right Livelihood** - Earning a living without harming

others; avoiding trades in weapons, living beings, meat, alcohol, and poison

Mental Discipline (Samadhi)

6. **Right Effort** - Cultivating wholesome qualities while preventing unwholesome ones; balanced spiritual energy

7. **Right Mindfulness** - Mental awareness and clarity in all activities; mindful attention to body, feelings, mind, and phenomena

8. **Right Concentration** - Developing focus through meditation; training the mind for clarity and insight

Key Buddhist Terms & Concepts

Guanyin - The Buddhist Goddess of Mercy and Compassion

- One of the most beloved figures in Chinese Buddhism
- Often depicted as female, though originally male in Indian Buddhism
- "Hears the cries of the world" and comes to aid suffering beings
- Represents the compassionate aspect of enlightenment

Bodhisattva - "Enlightenment Being"

- One who seeks enlightenment not just for themselves but to help all beings escape suffering
- Postpones their own final liberation to serve others
- Ji Gong embodies this ideal through his engaged compassion

Xuanzang - Historical Tang Dynasty monk (602-664 CE)

- Famous for his journey to India to collect Buddhist scriptures
- Traveled the Silk Road, facing incredible dangers
- His scholarly work helped establish Buddhism in China
- Referenced as example of dedication to spreading dharma

Dharma - Buddhist teaching and cosmic law

- The truth about the nature of existence
- Both the Buddha's specific teachings and universal principles
- "Living the dharma" means embodying these truths in daily life

Sangha - The Buddhist community

- Originally referred to monks and nuns
- Extended to include all Buddhist practitioners
- Represents the importance of spiritual community and mutual support

Karma - The law of cause and effect

- Actions (physical, verbal, mental) have consequences that shape future conditions
- Not fatalism, but moral responsibility for our choices
- Creates the conditions for rebirth and liberation

Samsara - The cycle of birth, death, and rebirth

- Driven by karma and desire

- Characterized by suffering and impermanence
- Liberation (nirvana) means escape from this cycle

Three Refuges - Taking refuge in the Buddha (teacher), Dharma (teaching), and Sangha (community)

- Central ceremony for becoming Buddhist
- Daoji receives these when becoming a monk
- Represents commitment to the Buddhist path

Buddhist Meditation & Practice

Mindfulness (Sati) - Careful attention to present-moment experience

- Awareness of thoughts, feelings, sensations without judgment
- Ji Gong practices this through engaged attention to others' needs

Loving-kindness (Metta) - Cultivation of unconditional friendliness

- Extends compassion even to enemies
- Key to Ji Gong's ability to transform former bandits

Right View - Understanding the true nature of reality

- Seeing through illusions of separateness
- Recognizing the interconnectedness of all life

PART II: CHINESE CULTURE & SOCIETY

Social Hierarchy in Song Dynasty China

Traditional Chinese society was structured in four main classes:

- **Scholars** - Educated administrators and officials
- Highest social status due to Confucian emphasis on learning
- Prepared for imperial examinations to become government officials
- Wei Sin represents this class and its transformation
- **Farmers** - Producers of food
- Considered essential to society's survival
- Higher theoretical status than merchants, despite less wealth
- Stone represents this class among the bandits
- **Artisans** - Craftspeople and skilled workers
- Valued for their practical skills and creativity
- Iron Wolf and Li Hua represent this class
- Included everything from blacksmiths to silk weavers
- **Merchants** - Traders and businesspeople
- Lowest in official hierarchy despite often being wealthy
- Suspected of profiting without producing
- Master Zhao represents this class

Confucian Values vs. Buddhist Ideals

Confucian Emphasis:

- Social harmony through proper relationships and roles
- Hierarchy based on education, age, and position
- Filial piety (respect for parents and ancestors)
- Government by virtuous, educated officials
- Preservation of tradition and cultural continuity

Buddhist Alternative (as presented by Ji Gong):

- Compassion transcends social boundaries
- All beings deserve equal respect and care
- Individual conscience over social conformity
- Service to suffering beings as highest virtue
- Transformation through understanding and love

Daily Life in Song Dynasty China

Architecture & Living Spaces

- Courtyard houses with central open spaces
- Multiple generations living together
- Separate quarters for different family functions
- Gardens as expressions of harmony with nature

Food Culture

- Rice as staple grain in the south
- Tea culture beginning to flourish

- Elaborate preparation and presentation of meals
- Seasonal and regional variations

Religious Practice

- Syncretism: Buddhism, Confucianism, and Taoism coexisted
- Ancestor veneration in family shrines
- Temple festivals and community celebrations
- Personal devotional practices

Economic Life

- Growing merchant class and trade networks
- Sophisticated monetary system
- Guilds controlling various crafts and trades
- Government regulation of commerce

Imperial Examination System

Purpose & Structure

- Meritocratic system for selecting government officials
- Based on classical Confucian texts
- Multiple levels from local to imperial
- Created educated bureaucratic class

Cultural Impact

- Made education highly valued throughout society
- Created common cultural knowledge among elites

- Sometimes divorced learning from practical application
- Scholar Wen represents both its strengths and limitations

PART III: HISTORICAL CONTEXT

Southern Song Dynasty (1127-1279)

Historical Background

- Founded when northern China fell to Jin Dynasty invaders
- Capital moved south to Hangzhou (then called Lin'an)
- Period of military weakness but cultural flowering
- Emphasized trade and commerce over military expansion

Ji Gong's Lifetime (1130-1209 CE)

- Born during the dynasty's early struggles
- Lived through period of relative stability and prosperity
- Witnessed the height of Song cultural achievement
- Died before the Mongol invasions that would end the dynasty

Hangzhou as Capital

- Became one of the world's largest cities
- Center of trade, especially silk production
- Known for natural beauty and cultural sophistication
- Setting allows Ji Gong to encounter all levels of society

Buddhism in Song China

Institutional Buddhism

- Well-established religion with imperial support
- Temples served as centers of learning and social welfare
- Monks expected to follow strict rules of conduct
- Accumulated significant wealth and political influence

Challenges & Tensions

- Debate over worldly involvement vs. spiritual withdrawal
- Tension between preserving doctrine and adapting to local needs
- Competition with Confucianism for cultural influence
- Corruption and institutionalization of some temples

Chan (Zen) Buddhism

- Emphasis on direct experience over textual study
- Less concerned with ritual, more with practical wisdom
- Ji Gong represents this tradition of engaged Buddhism
- Influenced by Taoist ideas about naturalness and spontaneity

Economic & Social Changes

Commercial Revolution

- Expansion of trade networks throughout Asia
- Development of paper money and credit systems

- Growth of urban centers and merchant class
- Increased social mobility through commerce

Technological Advances

- Improvements in agriculture and manufacturing
- Better transportation and communication
- Innovations in printing and scholarship
- Military technologies that couldn't prevent northern invasions

Social Tensions

- Growing wealth gaps between classes
- Pressure on traditional hierarchies from new wealth
- Tension between imperial ideology and local realities
- Corruption in government and religious institutions

PART IV: LITERARY & ARTISTIC TRADITIONS

Classical Chinese Poetry

Characteristics

- Highly valued art form requiring years of study
- Strict formal requirements (meter, tone, parallelism)
- Often expressed philosophical or emotional insights
- Marker of education and cultural refinement

Du Fu (712-770 CE)

- Tang Dynasty poet mentioned in the novel
- Known for social consciousness and technical mastery
- Wrote about war, poverty, and human suffering
- Model for combining artistic skill with moral vision

Role in Education

- Poetry composition required for imperial examinations
- Demonstrated cultural sophistication and moral character
- Used to express ideas indirectly during politically sensitive times
- Shared cultural vocabulary among educated classes

Calligraphy as Art Form

Techniques & Training

- Writing considered a high art form requiring years of practice
- Precise brush control and aesthetic sense essential
- Different styles for different purposes and moods
- Both practical skill and spiritual discipline

Cultural Significance

- Marker of education and cultural refinement
- Expression of personality and artistic vision
- Connection between physical practice and mental cultivation

- Bridge between literature and visual art

Games & Entertainment

Weiqi - "Go"

- Strategic board game of territory control
- Considered one of the "Four Arts" of Chinese scholars
- Metaphor for complex planning and strategy
- Required long-term thinking and adaptability

Other Pursuits

- Music (especially qin, a seven-stringed zither)
- Painting (landscape and calligraphy)
- Xiangqi or Chinese chess, and other strategy games
- Storytelling and folk entertainment

PART V: UNDERSTANDING JI GONG'S REVOLUTIONARY APPROACH

Traditional vs. Engaged Buddhism

Traditional Monastery Life:

- Withdrawal from worldly concerns to focus on enlighten-ment
- Strict adherence to rules (no alcohol, meat, etc.)
- Preservation of doctrine and institutional continuity

- Personal purification through disciplined practice

Ji Gong's Engaged Buddhism:

- Active involvement in social problems and community needs
- Rules serve compassion, not institutional preservation
- Enlightenment through service to others, not personal advancement
- Living wisdom more important than preserving abstract knowledge

Why Ji Gong Was Controversial

Religious Concerns:

1. Broke monastic rules (drinking wine, eating meat, living among laypeople)
2. Challenged religious authority by acting on individual conscience
3. Blurred boundaries between sacred and secular life
4. Suggested that wisdom could exist outside formal religious training

Social Concerns:

1. Treated all people as equals, regardless of social class
2. Encouraged servants and workers to expect dignified treatment
3. Reformed criminals instead of punishing them according

to law
4. Created alternative community structures outside government control

Political Concerns:

1. Demonstrated that individual conscience could conflict with institutional authority
2. Showed that social transformation was possible without government initiative
3. Created loyalty to principles rather than persons or institutions
4. Threatened established order by proving alternatives could work

His Revolutionary Ideas

Spiritual Revolution:

- Wisdom should serve people, not preserve itself in institutions
- Compassion requires action in the world, not contemplation apart from it
- True spirituality breaks down barriers between people rather than creating them
- Enlightenment is found through engagement, not escape

Social Revolution:

- People can change if given hope and opportunity rather than punishment and fear

- Social transformation happens through changed hearts, not changed laws
- Community based on mutual care is more stable than hierarchy based on control
- True authority comes from service to others, not power over them

Personal Revolution:

- Individual conscience sometimes must override social expectations
- Authentic living requires risk and often involves sacrifice
- Love is stronger than fear as a motivating force
- Everyone has the capacity for goodness if it's nurtured rather than suppressed

PART VI: THEMES FOR MODERN READERS

Universal Questions Explored

Institutional vs. Individual Conscience

- When do institutions serve their original purpose vs. preserving themselves?
- How do authentic individuals change corrupt or rigid systems?
- What's the relationship between personal spirituality and organized religion?
- When is it necessary to break rules to serve higher princi-

ples?

Social Justice & Personal Responsibility

- Can compassion be practical as well as idealistic?
- How do we balance individual needs with community welfare?
- What's the role of forgiveness in social transformation?
- How do we address systemic problems through personal action?

Authority & Power

- What's the difference between authority based on position vs. authority based on wisdom?
- How do we resist unjust power while remaining non-violent?
- What happens when official law conflicts with moral law?
- How do we create change without destroying valuable traditions?

Contemporary Relevance

Religious Life:

- Tension between institutional preservation and authentic spiritual practice
- Question of whether religious organizations serve God/truth or themselves
- Role of individual conscience in religious communities
- Balance between tradition and adaptation to current needs

Social Issues:

- Criminal justice: punishment vs. rehabilitation
- Economic inequality and social responsibility
- Treatment of refugees, immigrants, and marginalized people
- Community building across class and cultural lines

Personal Development:

- Finding authentic path vs. following expectations
- Balancing career success with meaningful contribution
- Courage to act on convictions despite social pressure
- Transforming personal pain into service to others

Political Engagement:

- Peaceful resistance to unjust systems
- Building alternative communities and structures
- Working within vs. outside established institutions
- Individual responsibility for social problems

PART VII: DISCUSSION QUESTIONS

For Book Clubs & Study Groups

Character Development:

1. How does Li Xiuyuan's transformation into Ji Gong

reflect universal patterns of spiritual awakening?

2. What role does suffering play in the spiritual development of various characters?

3. How do different characters represent different approaches to social responsibility?

Cultural Understanding:

1. How do the conflicts between Buddhist and Confucian values reflect tensions in any society?

2. What can modern readers learn from Song Dynasty approaches to education, governance, and community?

3. How does the novel's portrayal of Chinese Buddhism differ from Western stereotypes?

Philosophical Themes:

1. Is Ji Gong's approach to Buddhism authentic or a distortion of traditional teaching?

2. How does the novel address the tension between individual conscience and social stability?

3. What's the relationship between personal transformation and social change in the story?

Modern Applications:

1. How might Ji Gong's methods apply to contemporary social problems?

2. What institutions in our society might benefit from Ji Gong's approach to reform?

3. How do we balance respect for tradition with the need

for change and adaptation?

For Educational Settings

Historical Context:

- Research the actual historical Ji Gong and compare with the novel's portrayal
- Investigate Song Dynasty China's contributions to world civilization
- Explore the role of Buddhism in Chinese cultural development

Comparative Religion:

- Compare Buddhist concepts of compassion with similar ideas in other religions
- Examine different approaches to monasticism across world religions
- Analyze the relationship between mystical experience and social action

Literary Analysis:

- Examine the novel's use of historical fiction to explore contemporary themes
- Analyze character development techniques and symbolic elements
- Compare this work with other novels about spiritual transformation

PART VIII: FURTHER READING & EXPLORATION

Primary Sources

- **The Lotus Sutra** - Foundational Mahayana Buddhist text
- **The Heart Sutra** - Short but essential Buddhist wisdom text
- **Analects of Confucius** - Core Confucian teachings on ethics and governance

Historical Ji Gong

- **The Mad Monk: Ji Gong** by B.E.F. Rea - Academic study of the historical figure
- Traditional Chinese folk tales and opera about Ji Gong
- Scholarly articles on Song Dynasty Buddhism

Chinese Buddhism

- **The World of Chinese Buddhism** by Holmes Welch
- **Buddhism in Chinese Society** by Kenneth Ch'en
- **The Practice of Chinese Buddhism** by Holmes Welch

Song Dynasty History

- **Daily Life in China on the Eve of the Mongol Invasion** by Jacques Gernet
- **The Song Dynasty in China** by Yoshinobu Shiba
- **Life and Society in Song Dynasty China** by Christopher Cullen

Buddhist Philosophy

- **What the Buddha Taught** by Walpola Rahula - Clear introduction to core concepts
- **The Heart of Buddhist Meditation** by Nyanaponika Thera
- **Engaged Buddhism** by Thich Nhat Hanh - Modern application of Buddhist principles

Comparative Spirituality

- **The Perennial Philosophy** by Aldous Huxley
- **The Hero with a Thousand Faces** by Joseph Campbell
- **Mysticism** by Evelyn Underhill

This companion guide is meant to enhance, not replace, the reading experience. The story itself contains all the wisdom necessary for understanding Ji Gong's transformative journey.

About the Author

E ric M. Attio is a master of unexpected transformations, much like the characters he creates.

A New York native who found his creative voice in the sun-soaked landscapes of Florida over two decades ago, Eric inhabits the fascinating intersection where practical wisdom meets mystical imagination. By day, he navigates the complex human dramas of real estate, helping families find their perfect homes. But his sixteen years as an admissions counselor first taught him the art of reading between the lines of human stories, discovering the extraordinary dreams hiding within ordinary applications.

Eric's journey into authorship began with a simple but powerful philosophy: follow your highest excitement. What started as writing stories purely for his own joy became an irresistible compulsion to share these visions with the world. His theatrical background (acting in films and theater, producing and directing Off-Broadway) instilled in him a deep understanding of character, dialogue, and dramatic tension. Combined with his comic editing experience, this performance background sharpened his eye for visual storytelling, pacing, and the electric moment when words leap off the page. His diverse professional experiences with thousands of life stories deepened his understanding of what makes people tick and what makes them transcend their circumstances.

Drawing from his philosophy of practical mysticism, Eric creates genre-bending narratives that refuse to be contained by conventional boundaries. Whether exploring the depths of historical China, the far reaches of speculative futures, or the shadowy corners of contemporary mysteries, his work is united by a singular vision: revealing the profound within the mundane, the sacred within the secular, and the magical within the everyday.

His literary yet accessible style invites readers on journeys that are both intellectually satisfying and emotionally resonant: stories that entertain while they enlighten, that thrill while they transform. In Eric's fictional worlds, meticulous research meets boundless imagination, creating narratives where anything is possible and everything matters.

Eric M. Attio doesn't just write books; he crafts doorways to wonder.